THE HANGMAN'S JOURNAL

SHASHI WARRIER

SPEAKING TIGER

SPEAKING TIGER BOOKS LLP
125 A, Ground Floor, Shahpur Jat
New Delhi–110049, India

First published in hardback as *Hangman's Journal*
by Penguin Books India 2000
First published in paperback by Penguin Books India 2009
Th is edition published in paperback as *Th e Hangman's Journal*
by Speaking Tiger 2016

ISBN: 978-93-85755-80-4
eISBN: 978-93-85755-81-1

10 9 8 7 6 5 4 3 2 1

Typeset in Adobe Caslon Pro by Jojy Philip
Printed at Sanat Printers, Kundli

SHASHI WARRIER was born in 1959 and, after completing a Master's degree in economics, tried his hand at many professions that had nothing to do with economics. He progressed in fits and starts through journalism, consulting, computer software, project management and so on, and then settled down to write. Shashi Warrier is the author of the novels *Night of the Krait*, *Sniper* and *The Girl Who Didn't Give Up*, among others. He has also written two books for children, *The Hidden Continent* and *Suzy's Gift*.

He likes yoga, motorcycles, Hindustani music and good thrillers, and has been learning to cook for the past six years with little success. His most memorable achievement has been a solo forty-day 11,000 km motorbike ride around India. He now lives in Mangalore, not far from a beach, with his painter-writer wife Prita, their three dogs and two cats.

~

Praise for *The Hangman's Journal*

'One could expect a book such as this to be a prurient catalogue of crime and punishment: what each man did; how he died; and what he did as he died. Astonishingly, [the hangman] Pillai tells us practically none of those ... his journal is a stark, spare meditation on what it means to have led a life such as his ...The prologue of *The Hangman's Journal* rivals in its tenebrous brilliance the beginning of Michel Foucault's *Discipline and Punish: The Birth of the Prison* with its eyewitness account of a public execution ... [but] neither Pillai nor Warrier is interested in Hanging as a defining moment in any History of Reason. They are both storytellers, and as such tell a complexly interwoven moral tale of a life recollected in much intranquility ... [T]he arrival of this remarkable book is to be welcomed.'

—*Indian Review of Books*

'A sophisticated investigation into the nature of morality and the shifting nature of reality ... There is a moment where the ageing narrator, the hangman, recalls a deep-rooted memory of the steps leading up to the gallows: "In my mind that spot is very clearly visible, for there are the marks of feet all the way up to it, but none leading away." It is this almost chilling perception of loss and of a man's lifelong dilemma torn between duty and morality that is the underlying theme of this delicate novel written with unwavering sincerity ... [*The Hangman's Journal*] is a fascinating and at the same time unsettling account of a complex life, written with an assurance and a delicacy that is unusual for such an uncomfortable theme. This is a novel that deserves to be on the bookshelf of every discerning reader.'

—The National

'Warrier, mixing fact with fiction, traces the innermost life and thoughts of a man whose daily business was the business of death ... *The Hangman's Journal* does not set out to evoke any sympathy. Instead, it places the sequence of events in a rather unusual life where there were no friends and no foes. There was only the overwhelming stench of death.'

—The Hindu

'With [*The Hangman's Journal*] Shashi Warrier ... has achieved something genuinely impressive: A fictional portrait of a real person that never compromises the facts, and a novel that deftly walks the tightrope between reality and myth. The result is a haunting and provocative story that brings the reader inside the head of a man who fuels his existence, and that of his family, with death.'

—Irish Examiner

'Thought-provoking, harrowing, and lingers long in the mind.'

—Mail on Sunday

'This dark but unforgettable tale ... marks Warrier's breakthrough into the ranks of top Indo-English talents.'

—The Week

This book is dedicated to my late uncle, Dr P.S. Warrier, without whose support it would not have been written. I only wish he had lived to see its completion.

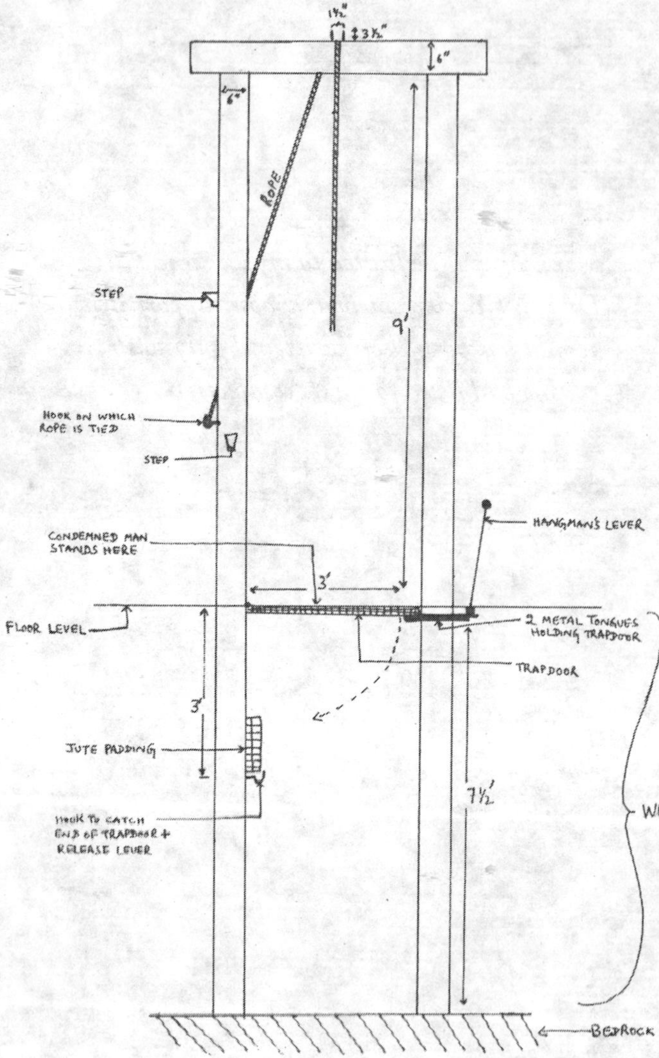
1½"
3½"
6"
6"
ROPE
STEP
HOOK ON WHICH ROPE IS TIED
STEP
9'
HANGMAN'S LEVER
CONDEMNED MAN STANDS HERE
3'
FLOOR LEVEL
2 METAL TONGUES HOLDING TRAPDOOR
TRAPDOOR
3'
JUTE PADDING
7½'
HOOK TO CATCH END OF TRAPDOOR + RELEASE LEVER
WELL
BEDROCK

Prologue

'They call it the drop.

'The warders have a little table for it, to tell you what distance the condemned man must fall with the noose around his neck, for him to die cleanly. Experts say that he must fall just enough to gather sufficient momentum for the rope to break his neck. If the body falls too far, the rope cuts into the neck and might even sever the head. If the body doesn't fall far enough, the neck won't break and the man will die of strangulation, taking several minutes over it. So the heavier the man, the shorter the drop.

'I know the table by heart. If the man weighs under 44 kilos, he should drop 1.98 metres. If he weighs between 44 and 57 kilos, the drop should be 1.83 metres. Between 57 and 70 kilos, the drop comes down to 1.68 metres. And a man weighing over 70 kilos need drop only 1.52 metres.

'It's hard to think of it as a table like this. The British

worked it out as a rule of thumb: I think it was a drop of six and a half feet for a man weighing a hundred pounds, and six inches less for every thirty pounds extra weight. When they converted the measurements into kilograms and centimetres the table changed to these clumsy numbers that we have now. I am uncomfortable with centimetres and kilograms I prefer to use the pounds and inches, they taught me at school.

'The precision of the table is misleading. To get the drop exactly right, you need to know the height of the knot, the height of the beam over which the rope is passed, and the length of the drop itself. And when you have measured the height of the condemned man, you must subtract from it the length of his head. But they don't do all that. They don't even weigh the man just before hanging him; they weigh him once a month while he is in the condemned cell.

'But no hangman worth his salt needs the table, or a weighing scale, or a measuring tape. He can guess the weight of the man to within five pounds, and then work out the length of the drop to within an inch.

'Measuring out the rope is easy: one span of my right hand is exactly eight and a half inches. I use that to measure off the required length. The horizontal beam from which the man hangs is a little over nine feet—thirteen hand-spans—above the trapdoor. To that I add one hand-span or more, depending on the condemned man's size, for the slack in the rope needed to ensure that the man's head stops just below the level of the trapdoor at the end of his fall. Since I can guess a man's height to an inch and his weight to a pound, the rest is easy.

'With a very heavy man, especially a tall one, I make the drop longer than the book says. Everyone who has seen me hanging a tall man will know this. According to the book, a six-footer weighing 70 kilos need drop only five feet. But if a tall man falls only five feet, his head will be visible above the trapdoor afterwards, and that I cannot bear to think about. The face is hidden behind a mask of cloth, of course, but I have seen a man's tongue swelling behind the mask. That is why I make sure that a tall man always has a little extra slack, and that is why the warders, who know this, do not protest.

'I know these lengths so well that a look at the condemned man suffices; I can do the rest blindfolded.

'Measuring out the rope, testing it, tying the knots—I do these things well. I have learnt to do them well because I concentrate on them as best I can, because if I don't my mind will find its way to the man about to die, and then I will have no peace …'

The letter came on a wet August morning as I sat reading this passage for the twenty-fifth time. It was a cheap yellow postcard with a single line in Tamil, a language that I had only recently begun to learn. I read very slowly, but the message was clear at first glance. 'Come immediately,' it said. The name was familiar, as was the address at the bottom of the postcard, but the handwriting was strange.

That address was the home of the hangman, who lived some four hundred kilometres south, in another state. I hadn't heard from him in a while and our last meeting had been stormy. I had returned from his home and written off the project on which we had been working together since sometime in the summer.

And now this letter. It was in someone else's handwriting. What had happened to the old man?

'Come immediately.' It was just short of eleven, and there was a train at half-past-two. If I took that train I'd be there late, towards midnight. I sat thinking and looking at the wet hillside for another hour, then went inside to pack and eat.

Before I left I made a telephone call to a lady several hundred kilometres away, to tell her about the letter.

'What will you do?' she asked.

'I'm on my way,' I said.

'Do you want me along?'

'Not yet,' I replied. 'But if the going gets heavy I'll call you.'

She had been on the project ever since the beginning, and had even pushed me along when I was on the verge of giving it up.

'Call me as soon as you know what's happening,' she said.

It was nearly one when I left, and I made it just in time to Shoranur railway station. The hours passed. The rain died out and people in the train opened the windows to let in the cool, damp air. At night the moon appeared briefly between clouds sliding smoothly north east, and glinted off ponds with reeds waving on their banks.

And all the while I wondered whether the hangman had kept his word. I wouldn't know until I got there. Time passed slowly.

I saw him in my mind's eye as I had seen him last: a man of average height for those parts, some five feet five inches tall, with long wavy grey hair and a grey beard that reached midway down his chest. He was thin, with a prominent nose that stuck out of his face like a cleaver, and a hangdog expression about him that was somehow engaging. He was dressed in a clean but shabby white shirt with a saffron lungi knotted about his waist. His hands were those of a bigger man, the thick strong fingers like knobbly tree roots. His feet were bare and rough, and one look at them told you that he had always been barefoot.

The image faded. How could I have believed that such a man would write a book?

There was a bus ready and waiting when the train reached Trivandrum at about ten, and at that time of the night we made good time to the temple town of Nagercoil, just short of the Cape. I found a small, cheap hotel and fell exhausted into bed. For all the weariness, though, sleep didn't come. The same question kept pounding in my head through the night: had the hangman kept his word? I wouldn't know till morning.

I woke before the dawn and lay restless and tossing, impatient to reach the hangman. At eight I took a bus to Parvathipuram, getting off at a small junction where a canal flows under crossroads.

The rain began again and I brought the umbrella out of my backpack. The wind whipped spray all over my trousers as I squelched through the mud without a qualm. All along the way the earth seemed to burst with life. Weeds grew thickly on both sides of the path, and in the paddy fields little shoots stuck tender heads above rippling muddy water. Wet banana leaves gleamed even in the cloud-dimmed light of the grey morning, and the birds kept silent.

The hangman's house, when I reached it, seemed smaller and quieter than it had been the last time I came. The old dog in the yard was gone, and when the gate squeaked open the face that appeared at the door wasn't the hangman's but his son's.

He nodded at me, but when I reached the door the welcome ended. 'You must have got my letter,' he said. I could see he wasn't enthusiastic about having me around. There was a hint of anger in his dark eyes.

'I got it yesterday and started immediately.'

He nodded again. 'Amma wanted to write you as soon as it happened but I thought it better to let you know only later.'

'As soon as what happened?' I asked. The pounding of my heart was louder. What was this man talking about?

'Appa's passing.' The anger in his eyes intensified.

I went cold all over. Here it was, the end. He had died before he could keep his promise. Stupid, I said to myself, I should have followed up earlier. There was a new weight in my chest. 'I'm sorry,' I said. 'How did he go? When?'

'He died two weeks ago ... in the morning. He woke up, had his coffee and lay down in the middle of the morning and never woke up again.'

'Did he suffer?'

'No. He just lay down to sleep and never got up again ... Amma found him—'

Almost as if on cue she appeared around the corner of the house, asking, 'Who's there?' She saw me and hesitated. I noticed she was dressed in white. Widow's white.

'I found out only just now,' I told her. 'I'm sorry. I would have liked to have been here for the last rites.'

Her eyes were red and heavy but the worst of her grief was past. She nodded. 'At least he went quietly,' she said. 'No trouble.' Suddenly there were fresh tears in her eyes and she wiped them away with a dark, bony hand. She told me what he had said when he woke up on his last morning, and pointed out the spot where he had sat to drink his coffee. She showed me the worn shirt he had taken off before he lay down for the last time. She spoke of the quiet in his eyes in his last few days. She showed me where they had cut down a tree for the wood to cremate him, and told me which neighbours had come first when they heard her wails. She spoke of him sometimes as if he were still alive, and I listened patiently.

When she was through, she turned to her son, her youngest child. 'Did you give him the packet?' she asked.

He shook his head. 'He had just arrived when you came and started talking to him,' he said.

She was angry. 'How can you keep him waiting at the door like this? Give him his packet. That's what you called him for, isn't it?'

The son disappeared into the darkness of the house, grumbling, and she turned to me. 'He was happy when he went. He left something for you. He told us to give it to you.' She paused. 'Those books of yours. He was busy with them all along. He said he was finished with them, that he would send them to you in a day or two, but he was gone before he could do that.'

The son reappeared with a large yellow plastic bag in his hands. In it were notebooks, seven of them, and a pen. I reached inside to pick out the pen. 'This is for you,' I said, offering it to them. 'I gave it to him.'

The widow smiled and shook her head. 'What will we do with it? Besides, he said it's for you. He said that everything in the bag is for you. It's yours.'

'Thank you. Where's his dog?'

'He's also gone. A few days ago, in his sleep. He too just lay down quietly and never got up again.'

I nodded. There was a lump in my throat, but I couldn't wait to get back to the hotel room and see what was in those notebooks. She must have sensed my impatience. 'Go,' she said. 'Go on. Read the books. Do well.'

Out of the corner of my eye I saw the son looking resentfully at me. I put the books and the pen in my pack and turned and walked away. I opened the gate and stepped out into the slush that was the road. At the corner I turned, and saw the two of them, mother and son, standing still, watching me. I lifted a hand in a wave and they waved back. Then the rain came heavily down and I never saw them again.

Back in the hotel room I started on the notebooks. There were seven of them, all numbered in English in his sprawling childish hand. The contents were in Tamil. I could just barely read the language, but I started immediately. There were words that I couldn't understand, but I got the general drift of the journal very quickly. Some of it I'd read before, and that made it easier. Later I'd get my friend, the lady who had helped me with the project, to translate the notes for me.

The hangman had written his notes as neatly as he could. His writing became a little smoother as he wrote, but not much: you can't expect the hand of a man of seventy-four to improve dramatically. It was mostly a journal, a diary, and in it he had put down some of the matters that weighed most upon his mind.

This is what I read.

1

They came at the worst possible time, at two on an afternoon in late April when the summer's sun was getting to be its pitiless worst.

Chellammal, my wife, was away at a friend's house: she comes and goes as she pleases, and I stopped interfering with her long ago because she does as she wants anyway. There was never anything in my house to steal, just a few pots and pans and clothes and sticks of furniture, so I left the door open always. I was alone in the backyard, looking at the parched fields, at the soil caking hard and cracking with thirst. Beside the fields, a coconut plantation and a mango orchard, both retaining their green cover, gave an illusion of lushness from above. But when you looked closely the soil underneath was bone dry, its moisture sucked out by the hungry sun.

Despite the harsh heat I was smoking a beedi, my fifth of the day: these small vices make an old man's summer bearable. My dog, a stray that had walked into the yard one night some years ago, came skulking up to my side. He was thick-limbed and stiff with age, but still strong, though his eyes were beginning to go. He lay at my feet with a small grunt of satisfaction, panting hard, his tongue out.

In the stillness of the afternoon there was little noise: the heat brings with it a terrible sluggishness that affects everything that lives—the cattle, the dogs, and even the kites that drift high above. As for me, I don't sleep much. There was little I could do but sit still, too lethargic to do anything, but unable to doze off. It's an old man's habit.

I sat in the warm shade and let my mind drift. Sometimes when something happens, you think you will never forget it. You think you will never forget your wedding, for instance, but I've forgotten … I've forgotten even what my wife looked like on our wedding day, and on the rare occasions I look at my wedding photographs I think it's a pair of strangers in there. I've forgotten the day I first went to school, though I remember one of the schoolmasters very well. My memory is unpredictable, for sometimes the smallest of incidents lingers on in my mind far longer than it should. I still remember, for instance, the call of the raven from high above when we were doing the last rites for my father, but I don't remember my father's face clearly. Sometimes my memory irritates me: I remember a face in great detail, features and wrinkles and all, but can't put a name to it or even recall the context in which I saw it.

So these random memories were all I lived with, and I had grown fond of them, for though they betrayed me once in a while they were my only friends ... How true they were was another matter.

These memories and an approaching blackness—a sort of heavy blackness, I often wondered what it was. Was it the sadness that caught my father when he was past seventy, as I am now? I wondered, though I had felt it since I was sixty.

I heard the car from far away, a distant hum that grew and sometimes stopped, perhaps when they paused to ask for directions. The sound interrupted my thoughts, which took a long time to get back together. This made the people in the car intruders, whoever they were. Who were they, anyway, I thought, and whom did they want to meet? My neighbours are poor, as am I; we have nothing to do with wealthy people who have cars. Who would want to visit one of us?

A few minutes later I heard the car stop and the doors slam shut. There were voices then, a man and a woman, speaking in English, a language that I can recognize but don't understand. They seemed to be nearby, so I went slowly around my small two-room house, the dog following stiffly, and found at my gate two young strangers. The man was tall and fat and bearded and bespectacled, the woman thin and fair-skinned, with red lips. As I watched, the dog went up to the woman, who was leading, and began to sniff at her skirt.

She did not fear him. She bent and patted his head, scratching him behind his ears, just where he likes to be scratched. He grunted in pleasure and went still. She straightened up, looking hesitantly at me. 'Do you know where Janardhanan Pillai lives?' she asked in Tamil. Her Tamil was chaste, the language of the wealthy, not the earthy sing-song that you hear around my house.

'Yes,' I replied. I answered the question but volunteered nothing.

She waited for a few seconds before she asked, 'Where does he live, then?'

I pointed at the small whitewashed house with the thatch roof. 'Here.'

'Janardhanan Pillai? The aratchar?'

'Yes,' I said. 'The aratchar. He lives here.'

She looked me up and down, and hesitated again. 'Do you know him?' she asked.

I couldn't evade anymore. 'I am him,' I replied.

Her tone changed a little, the relief showing. 'We come from far away,' she said. 'We have been looking for your house for most of the day ... We must have asked at a dozen places, disturbed a dozen others.'

'What do you want from me?' I asked. No one comes far unless they want something, and these people must have wanted it very badly, whatever it was, to come out here in the heat and on these bad roads.

She looked me in the eye. 'Words,' she said, briefly.

For the first time I felt a spark of curiosity. 'What words?' I asked.

'My friend is a writer,' she replied. 'He seeks your words.'

They must have prepared for this meeting. 'Why does he not speak for himself?' I asked. 'What man would have a woman speak for him?'

'A man who does not know the language,' she said. She smiled then, a smile of relief that I had not turned them away forthwith.

Some of my anger dissolved in that smile. I am old but when a beautiful young woman smiles at me I still respond. This one was a little too thin, and her face was painted, but she was still quite beautiful. 'What is his language, then?' I asked. 'Malayalam?' They speak Malayalam in Kerala, only forty kilometres away.

'He speaks Malayalam,' she said, 'but he writes in English.'

People like this had come before. They had taken photographs and they had written about me, most in Tamil, a few in Malayalam, and one or two in English. I had been happy and proud at first to see my face in the newspapers, to read about myself, but very soon it became unimportant, for they never said anything that mattered. 'From which newspaper?' I asked.

'None,' she replied. 'He wants to write a whole book about you.'

'A book.' The others had come and sat and talked for hours just to produce a quarter of a page in a newspaper. How much time of mine would this man take, I wondered, to write a book of a few hundred pages? But the idea was attractive.

Deep in my heart I had wanted all along to write a book. To write my own book. I had thought about my book for a quarter-century, but never put down a word. I had thought vaguely that there was enough in my mind for a good story. And always I had postponed writing it, not knowing why. Now, perhaps, the time had come to write it. And this man was there, for me to learn from.

'What will he call the book?' I asked.

'The Hangman's Journal,' she replied, 'The publishers suggested the name. It seems all right. He will write it as if you are writing it: a first-person narrative.'

'A book about me, written by a stranger half my age pretending to be me,' I repeated. It seemed funny, but I didn't think they'd see the humour. 'How long will it take?'

She didn't reply immediately. When you are as old as I am, and have seen a lifetime of lies, it is easy to tell when someone is lying to you. I saw the hesitation in her eyes, and then a decision to tell the truth. 'He will probably take six to eight months to write the book,' she explained.

'And will it be printed soon after that?'

She shook her head. Again there was the hesitation, followed by the truth. 'Perhaps six to eight months more. Perhaps a year.'

'Will it have my photograph on the cover?' Fifteen or twenty years ago it would have made a difference, but no longer. I had no desire to be in the public eye. All the same, I did want to know if these people would try to evade.

Again there was the hesitation, then the truth afterwards. 'I don't know.'

'And will he make a lot of money out of it?'

'He does not know,' she explained. 'Writing … If you write you must be prepared to be poor.'

'If he is poor, how does he have a car?'

'It's not his car,' she explained. 'It's mine. I like his writing, so I help him when I can.'

'And what are you to him?' I asked.

'An old friend who likes books, and a distant relative … I've known him since he was two.'

I looked more closely and suddenly I knew that the woman was older, though she didn't look it … They were colleagues of a sort. It seems very common these days. A few years ago a girl came, from a magazine. With her came a photographer, a young man. God knows what the world is coming to: in my youth you wouldn't see a man and a woman travelling together unless they were married. At least these two were related. 'So what will I get out of it?' I asked. Here they were, asking me to help with a book, a book yet to be written, saying that writing does not pay. What did they think they have which could persuade me to give them the words?

'I don't know,' she replied. 'I thought you would be pleased to have a book written about you … But he is willing to share the money that he will get for it.'

'What share?'

'Half for you. Half for him.'

They had prepared thoroughly for this meeting then, for she spoke without consulting him. Again it struck me that these two were very close, very close in mind, and then it didn't seem odd, their being here together. Half the money sounded good, but I knew that half of nothing is nothing. 'How much would that be?'

'Let me confirm with him,' she said. They spoke in English, and he nodded. Again she smiled.

'You'll get a minimum of five thousand rupees, maybe more.'

Five thousand for me was not bad, even if I had to spend a month with the writer. 'Is that all he gets?' I asked.

'He gets a royalty after that, some money for each book sold, but what he gets is adjusted against the advance.'

So it was possible that he wouldn't get anything after that advance. I looked carefully at the man. His clothes were poor, not much better than mine, cheap cotton. He was young, in his middle to late thirties. They both looked earnest, and they had taken a lot of trouble. But could I trust them? They would come and take my words and disappear. 'Only half?' I asked, playing for time. 'The words are mine, he just writes them down … And for that he gets half? That doesn't sound right.'

She turned to explain to him but he held up a hand: he knew enough to understand what I had said. I could see it in his eyes. He spoke, firmly and briefly, and she said to me, 'This book is not about money, he says. This is about your mind, your soul. If you are going to talk, you will talk regardless of the money.'

He was right: he could see that the money wasn't

important. Maybe he needed it more than I did. 'All right,' I said. 'Let's talk for a while. We'll decide later about whether I'll help with the book and how much money you pay me.' I paused. 'Let's go into the house.'

The man spoke again, bending towards the woman. An ordinary voice, as deep as one would expect from a man his size. She nodded at him, then turned to ask me, 'Would you mind sitting outside, in the shade?'

'As you wish,' I said. 'Why?'

'He wants to get a feel for the land,' she replied. 'He likes to sit and watch.'

'Why does he want to do that?'

'To get a sense of your origins, your background.'

'All right.' I didn't mind. From outside the interior of the house looked dark and deceptively cool; inside, it would be stifling. That was why I was outside in the first place. 'I'll get chairs.'

'Don't bother,' the woman said. 'We can sit there.' She pointed at a lump of concrete by the house.

So there we sat, me in the doorway and the two of them on the concrete, facing me. I saw the curiosity in his eyes then. In the eyes of the others there was reserve, and sometimes pity. In some there was awe, and in others horror. But in this man there was nothing but curiosity. He had come with an empty mind.

'So what do you want me to tell you?' I asked the man. It was clear that he understood simple Tamil, that the woman would interpret the long words and the nuances.

He spoke to the woman in English, and she turned

to me to ask, 'If the hundred and seventeen people you hanged could hear you today, what would you tell them?'

Strange question to start with. The others, the ones from the newspapers, asked about the rituals and the rope and how it was done, and added on at the end a question about how it felt. This man was starting with the heart of the matter. I thought in silence for a moment, but nothing surfaced in my mind. I have, after all, been asking myself this same question for the past quarter-century and have not yet found an answer. I shook my head. 'Later,' I said. 'Ask me something else now. I'll have to think about it.'

The man spoke in her ear, and she asked. 'Haven't you thought about it all along?'

Yes,' I smiled at their youth. 'Very little else, these past few years, since I retired.'

'Well ...' she said, cocking an eyebrow at me.

'For some questions you don't get easy answers. Ask me something else.'

They spoke again, and she said, 'But this is the most important question. Unless he has some kind of a beginning of an answer he won't be able to write the book.'

'Why not?' I asked, trying to draw him towards the circus of rituals. 'There was a lot of ritual in the old days.'

He tapped her wrist. I think he didn't understand the word I used for ritual. She explained to him, and he spoke a question to her. She shook her head at him, but then turned to me. 'He says he knows that you are the only one who knows about what it was in the days of the king, and afterwards. That is why he has come to you. He asks, from your point of view, did it make a difference?'

That was easy to answer. 'No,' I said. 'It made no difference who gave the orders, the king or the government that followed him.' After I'd said this, I felt that it wasn't entirely true, but I let it be.

She translated for him again. There was a smile on his face when he told her his question. She shook her head again, the bell of hair dancing about her head, and I heard him repeat himself. 'Difficult question,' she said to me. 'He says that if it made no difference who gave the orders, the rituals don't matter. Isn't that so?'

'That might be so,' I said, feeling trapped. 'Tell me, what do you really want from me?'

He understood that question. He spoke to her for some time, for nearly three minutes, as far as I could judge, with many gestures of his hands. He had restless hands, this one, but his eyes were very focused.

She heard him out in silence. 'He says he wants to look at your point of view on executions, on life. He has read a little of the ritual but is not satisfied. People in this country have looked into the minds of condemned men. They have looked into the minds of prison officials, and the judges who have delivered sentences of death. But no one has done that with the hangman. He wants to look into your mind and write a book about it.'

He was asking of me the hardest question of them

all. I didn't have the strength right then to speak to him. I rose from my doorstep and stretched. 'I'm tired now,' I told them. 'Let me think about things a little more.'

'When should we come next?' the man asked abruptly in his accented Tamil. His impatience showed.

'Where do you live?' I asked.

'In Nagercoil, for the time being,' she replied. 'On West Car Street, near the snake temple. I have relatives there, and so does he.'

'Come back in two days,' I said. 'And come in the morning. If you come in the morning I will be able to offer you coffee.'

'The day after tomorrow? About eleven in the morning?' he asked, still groping for the right word.

I liked that, the way he groped for words. He seemed like a man who tried hard to get things right. 'Yes,' I told him. 'The day after tomorrow. At eleven …'

2

I see the steps first, the irregular stone steps leading into the dark well below the trapdoor. All around is the soft darkness before the dawn, and a powdering of bright stars in the patches of sky above. There is light also from the powerful lamps all over the premises, the lamps that keep the night from taking over. From far away comes the sound of drums, rising and falling on a fugitive chill wind that I can feel on my cheek.

In the darkness of the well lurks something … a menace I cannot name. I turn from the well to look for reassurance in the familiar faces of my adiyaans, my mates, my assistants, who a few moments ago accompanied me into the gallows enclosure along with the guards, and the man in the mask.

They are gone. I am alone.

No, not quite alone. On the trapdoor, with the noose above him, stands the man in the mask. His striped uniform is crisp and fresh, and he stands very still. The rope is a clean bright white that seems to have a glow of its own. The knots at the man's ankles are neatly tied, compact—the work of someone who knows his ropes well. I cannot see his arms; they are tied behind him, as they should be. I have a vague memory of having tied those knots myself a long time ago. Some years ago.

There is something strange about the mask. The beat of the faraway drums rises and I see what is wrong. The mask is too flat. There should be at least one protuberance, where the man's nose sticks out, but on this mask there is none: it is flat. In a moment of insight I know that there is no face behind the mask.

The mask is the face.

The terror rises. I have to get away from here, from the hidden monster in the well and the faceless one on the trapdoor.

The solid iron door is less than thirty feet away, but I cannot run, no matter how hard I try. I move painfully slowly towards the door, but when I reach it I see that it is locked with a large padlock that I cannot even move. I go to the other door, the small one through which they pass the body to relatives waiting outside, but that too is locked with a similar padlock. I look at the walls around me: they are all at least twelve feet high, and smooth, offering no escape.

Some foreboding makes me turn around. And there is the man in the mask, the flat mask, his arms and legs free. I feel his hands tighten about my neck, powerful hands that I can't pry loose. I cannot breathe … I try to close my eyes and shut out the flat mask but I cannot. As I begin to sink to my knees my heart threatens to burst in my chest.

I came awake gasping for breath. It must have been a silent nightmare. Chellammal slept peacefully a few feet away. She normally snores mightily for such a small woman but that night she was silent, face-down.

It was stifling inside the house, and there were mosquitoes drifting in through the open windows. Not a breath of breeze stirred the leaves outside, and the world was still and black-and-silver, and strangely comforting. My torso was wet with sweat, as was the mat on which I was lying. I put my hands on the floor to raise myself; my body is much lighter than it had been in my youth, yet that night it felt much heavier. I moved slowly to the kitchen to get a drink of water from the pot on the shelf. I should have been able to find my way around this house blindfolded but I could not. I had to grope for the bolt at the top of the door, and it took all my remaining strength to slide it quietly down. It was too dark for me to see the time in the clock but I could tell from the quality of light outside that it was early morning: perhaps two. Three hours to dawn.

I went out with my mat. There was a slight shifting breeze, just enough to make you wish it wasn't there, because when it stops you are left miserable. I spread my mat on the ground in the open—they used to say in my childhood, never sleep under a tree at night—and stretched out to look at the stars.

Once I could see individual stars. Now I saw only dim glowing patches in the sky, that was all. I remember: in the nightmare the stars were sharp, as I saw them in the days when I ruled the gallows. It isn't just my eyes. My ears, too, have gone, and my nose—but that is because of the beedis, not old age.

I lay there and drifted back to the days when the stars were sharp in the sky and the smell of woodsmoke from the kitchen sharp in my nostrils. What did I think of in those days? There was a parade of memories, and the familiar blackness, but nothing else. I dreaded the prospect of the writer's visit. Why couldn't they leave me in peace? But I knew I couldn't turn them away. The writer asked the same question I asked myself. Several times I thought I knew the answer, but something happened that taught me that the answer was false.

The writer and the woman ... I felt a tinge of envy. In their talk I saw a closeness of mind. They shared their thoughts. I had lived longer than both of them put together but in all my life I'd had to keep everything to myself. Whom could I share with? A sense of desperate loneliness gripped me.

A book. That was attractive. Maybe I could pour it all out to the writer, the nightmares and the blackness and the disconnected bits of memory that an old man has.

The more I thought of it that dark morning, the more attractive the idea seemed.

When they come I will talk to them, I thought. There will be much in what I say that will be unclear, much that will be confused, much that will be repeated. Well, let the writer take care of all that. That is his job. The only thing that worried me was that he would write in English, a language I did not know. If he twisted anything I said and put it in his book, it would reflect on me and my sons. And what if the book told lies but I died before it was out? The only good side of it was that none of my people would know about the lies because none of them read books in English. But what if it did well and a translation came out?

Trust was difficult. Trusting a stranger was doubly difficult.

The nightmare came to mind, the man in the flat mask, with his hands at my throat. I had told no one about him. Would I dare tell anyone who cared to listen? Sharing secrets with strangers was difficult.

But I had never shared any of this even with those close to me, and I thought it might be worth trying.

I came to a decision then, in the breeze rising from the sea, that I would speak to the writer. The decision made, I lay back. And slept soundly through the rest of the night.

~

I awoke to the rooster's call, with the dawn in the sky. For a moment I was disoriented: what was I doing out here in the open? Then I remembered the nightmare, and getting out of the confines of the house, and the decision. I would speak to the writer one or two more times, to gauge the man, to see how deep he was willing to go. I would watch him closely. I thought then that he was devious, that he was using the woman to soften me up.

The morning was alive with the noise of birds. They went far in summer, searching for food and water. In the wet months finding sustenance was easy but in summer they had to struggle and they made a great deal of noise over it. A lone squirrel scurried up a tree-trunk and poked at the bark until he found himself a termite to eat. He sat holding it in both hands, nibbling at it, looking alertly at me, a large and unpredictable intruder in his universe.

He had his universe. I had mine. The writer had his.

I had tried, years ago, to give another man a look at my universe. I thought I had succeeded, but I hadn't, as I discovered later. Why, I have lived over half a century with Chellammal and there is much about her that I do not know. I know her habits and her grumbling and her watery snores at night, but beyond that she is a stranger.

Will everyone else always be a stranger to me?

By the time I finished my ablutions my breakfast was cold. It didn't matter: I learnt in childhood that cold food is better than no food. Be patient, chew it well, and it will go down easily. The coffee afterwards was hot and strong, with just a touch of sugar to take the edge off the bitterness, exactly the way I like it. After half a century together, Chellammal should know how to make my coffee.

I sometimes go visiting in the mornings. I have a younger brother staying close by, Paraman. Paraman is seven years younger, but he looks older because he never got married, never had a woman to look after him as my other brother and I did. Paraman is alone … I worry about him sometimes. He works when he feels like it, and gets by on very little.

I will go away at ten, I thought, and ask Chellammal to stay behind to tell the writer and his friend at eleven that they should wait. Let them cool their heels for an hour or so: then I will know how serious they are … But I knew they were serious. It wasn't fair, making them wait, and besides, I would lose time that way myself. No, I thought, I will be here at eleven. I will talk to them and decide whether or not to start on the book, whether or not I should share my life with them. I needed to unburden myself, and if I thought them fit I would unburden myself to them.

There was an urgency to the matter that I hadn't understood. Ever since I gave up my work a quarter-century ago, I had not hurried, or felt the need for hurry. But that day there was a feeling that I must do whatever I was doing quickly, an inner push that I could not ignore.

To quieten my restlessness I took a long walk. I didn't want to meet people, so I took off through the fields behind the house, hoping for solitude there. I found it, too: a few passers-by nodded their greetings but wouldn't stop to talk because they were hurrying to work. I used to walk around here regularly until about ten years ago. Then lots of houses came up and the walks lost their pleasure. That day I didn't notice the new houses, or the warmth of the early morning sun ... or the time passing. When I returned home it was a quarter-past-eleven and the youngsters were already there, the man with a tape-recorder and a notebook and a pen. When I saw them standing outside my house, leaning on the front of her car, heads close together, talking softly and earnestly, I felt again the pang of envy I had felt on their previous visit.

I was very tired then, after walking more than an hour in the fields. Chellammal saw me and began screaming at me. 'What do you mean by asking them to come here and going off without saying anything?' she asked in her rough, old-woman's voice. The man raised a hand with his palm outwards, mumbling something to her, perhaps that it didn't matter, and when I told her to keep quiet she went in grumbling to herself.

They sat again where they had sat before, side by side on the concrete, and I dragged out a chair for myself. The sun was bright in the sky, rising higher, and the breeze had died. They sweated even in the shade of the tree. 'Do you want to sit inside?' I asked.

The man got up and walked to the door to look inside. It's a humble house, one small room with a small enclosure to a side that is the kitchen. In the room are two cots, one bare, the other with a sheet stretched over it. It seems nicely dark inside, and cool, but that cool, as I have said before, is deceptive. He spoke to the woman, who explained, 'It's very small and we will be disturbing your wife. And there's no breeze inside. If you don't mind, let's stay here.'

'Do you want coffee?' I asked.

They nodded in unison, like twins. They were interested, they wanted to learn about me. They were well off, but they didn't seem to mind my poverty. I liked that very much. The others who came, they looked around, saw the small bare yard and the small cramped house—just one room and a kitchen, no bathroom, no toilet—and smelt the smell of manure coming in from the fields, and turned away to hide the pity in their eyes. But these two were different.

We sat quietly while Chellammal made coffee. 'Where do you get the money to live?' the writer asked as she brought three small tumblers of coffee.

I work occasionally, I get occasional presents from the extended family, and sometimes one of my sons or daughters helps with a little money. I get grain sometimes, after the harvests, as I used to before I retired. I also have an old-age pension. Life is difficult, but there's enough money for bare survival. I am as poor as I always was but others have become better off ... I must be one of the poorest in these parts, but it does not bother me. I didn't want to say all this to a stranger, so I simply said, 'I have a pension, and so does my wife. Enough.'

'All right,' he nodded.

I sipped the coffee. 'What do you want to know?' I asked.

He spoke to the woman, who translated. 'He wants to know how it is to kill someone.'

I shook my head. 'That's like his other question. I can't answer it quickly. Ask me something else.'

Again they spoke. The next question surprised me. 'How did the prison staff treat you?'

'With respect,' I said. That again was not strictly true.

He wouldn't give up. 'Always?' he asked.

There were some shameful recollections here. I found myself faltering. 'No,' I said, 'not always.'

'Why not?'

I evaded. 'I don't remember,' I said. 'My memory plays tricks with me.'

They sensed the evasion, and the discomfort that caused it. The man spoke to her, and she told me, 'This book is not going to be comfortable for you or for him. This is not going to be a circus, like those newspaper interviews. He wants you to know that.'

Didn't I know it? And what discomfort would *he* have to bear? They were *my* memories, weren't they? A wave of irritation rose. For a split second I wanted to tell them to leave and never come back. But it's hard to be irritated at people so earnest, and the anger fell back after a moment.

'Nonsense,' I said. 'What's to cause him discomfort? He just has to take what I tell him and clean it up.'

He spoke to the woman. 'He understands your discomfort,' she said. 'The choice is yours, you can talk to him or not. Whether he has a hard time with it or not doesn't matter.'

That was true. I was in my mid-seventies, without much time left, and this opportunity wouldn't come again. It wasn't much of a choice, actually. I'd have to trust these young people and go ahead with it. Thinking about the past was sometimes uncomfortable, and talking about it doubly so … 'Can you read Tamil?' I asked the woman.

'Yes,' she replied. 'Why?'

'Because it might be easier for me to write it. My own memories, in my own words.' I've never understood the impulse that made me say this, for I've never written more than a letter of a few lines after leaving school at the age of nine.

He interrupted, in his broken Tamil. 'I can suggest how we do it if you find it hard to talk about it.'

'What?' I asked.

He told her, and this is what she told me: 'You write whatever you like, and we'll come here every two weeks, read what you have written, ask you about it, and so on. You tell us the answers, or write them down, as you wish. We will keep doing this until you know us well enough to trust us.'

Trust. He knew exactly what was going on in my mind. He knew about trust. Maybe he was telling the truth about the book giving him as much discomfort as it gave me. 'We'll try that,' I said.

He spoke again, urgently. She nodded and said, 'He says please don't throw away anything that you write. It might not be of value to you but it might be useful to him.'

'Right,' I said. 'I'll throw away nothing … Unless it contains something that might hurt someone in my family.'

'Even then …' she began.

'I'll think about it,' I said, cutting her off.

He stood up from the lump of concrete, looking embarrassed. From his bag he drew a notebook, a large one with smooth ruled paper. From his pocket he took a dark blue pen, which looked like an expensive one. He held them out to me. 'Take these,' he said. 'This is a special pen. For a special person.'

I took the book and the pen. Experimentally I scrawled my name on the cover. Good smooth pen, good smooth paper. I looked up at him, found him smiling. He nodded. 'The pen is a gift for you. The book you fill in and give my friend, and we will read it and return it to you for keeping.'

Devious, devious man. Urging me on to write. He didn't trust me either. I'd do it, for my sake and not his, but he wasn't to know that. 'Come back in a few days,' I said. 'I'll have something ready for you in three days.'

'Saturday?' he asked.

'Saturday,' I confirmed. 'Same time.' I couldn't help smiling at their serious faces. 'Trust me.'

He smiled back, and there was a gleam of mischief in his eyes. 'Yes,' he said. 'I will.'

~

After they left I went into the house and put the notebook on a small low table. I sat on the floor by the table and looked at the blank page and couldn't find a word to write. Besides, it was too dark inside. I wanted to light a beedi but I never smoke inside the house because it is too small and the smell remains for a long while.

Chellammal began to nag at me. 'Why are you spoiling your eyes trying to write something that no one will read?' she grumbled as she sat in the doorway cutting beans for lunch. Beans with rice gruel and a little mango pickle, that is our usual lunch, and I could smell the gruel cooking. Sitting there amidst those sights and sounds and smells of the house I knew I wouldn't be able to write. I wanted to be alone. I needed to feel alone.

In the backyard, in the open, under a tree—that was best. It would also be a great deal brighter. So I rose and picked up the table. 'Where are you going?' she demanded. 'Have you become such a great writer that you won't speak even to your wife?' Her face used to take on a grim look at times like this, but of late she had been softer, ever since I fell ill three months earlier.

'I want to sit in the open,' I told her. 'In the backyard, where I can smoke without you nagging me.'

'It'll be hot,' she said, 'and you'll smoke too much.'

'So what if it's hot?' I asked. 'And you know that I'll smoke the same number of beedis whether I sit here or outside.'

She had something to say to that as well but I ignored her. She likes to talk while she's working and I didn't want to listen. I found a reasonably shady spot under the mango tree at the back and sat facing the fields.

The pen sat clumsily in my fingers and the words wouldn't come. I wished I had asked the writer how to begin, about how to get past the effort of writing the first word on a smooth sheet of paper. I remembered the first word anyone writes in a letter: Shri, in Sanskrit, the only Sanskrit I know.

Think first of the gods. My own gods are Bhadrakali, the deity to whom I prayed each time I was called upon to do my job, and Aiyyappan, in whose name I had gone to Sabarimala at least twenty times. I thought of both of them, and prayed a little, and still nothing happened. I thought of Ganesha, pot-bellied, with his trunk in the air, and still no words came.

Then I thought of the nightmare, and put it down.

When that was done, I thought of the prison, trying to picture it as it was over a quarter century ago, and at last the words came, slowly and painfully and clumsily. An image appeared in my mind. I decided to write about it, and moreover decided that I would write about it in a different fashion from the rest of this ... I didn't know what to call it, for it wasn't a book yet. It was a diary, a journal of sorts, so perhaps it was best to stick to the name they said in the beginning: The Hangman's Journal. That sounded nice. It came smoothly off the tongue, and I decided to ask the writer the words for it in English.

I would experiment with the picture in my mind. I would try to imagine it in my head, I would try to be in the picture that I described, and I would put down the words as they came. Since I would be in the picture I wrote about, it would be in the present tense, unlike the rest of the journal. I hoped the writer wouldn't find it too confusing. I didn't really know how intelligent he was, and how quickly he understood.

~

It is a mild winter's morning, with the sun just above the horizon and birdsong in the air. The mist is fading, and in the grass outside the porch the dewdrops glint orange and gold.

Around the ochre and grey buildings of brick and stone that is the prison complex is a large compound filled with trees, lush with the vegetation from the rains that still come and go, the clouds drifting in from the north, dark and heavy and brooding. All around the prison the world is coming alive to the new day, but behind me lies death.

As I emerge past the dark mouth of the prison entrance an ambulance goes slowly past. It is an old white Bedford with a tired engine that wheezes and pops, the red cross on its side faded with age, the glass behind dirty and almost opaque. The driver slouches in his seat: he has no need for his siren and flashing lights, no need to race to a hospital to save a life, for the man on the stretcher inside is already dead. His people are taking his body to the cremation ground. I get a glimpse of three men and a woman sitting quietly inside around the stretcher, their faces turned downwards: no weeping, no hysteria, just a silence. They don't look back at me as they go by, and for that I am relieved, for I killed the man an hour ago. I put the mask on his face and looped the white noose about his neck in the glare of the floodlamps on the tower, and tightened the knot until it sat just so. Then, with a prayer under my breath, I pulled the lever that operates the trapdoor, and down he went ... The rope quivered for a minute, and he was gone.

He was a young man, a young man who had killed two other young men three years earlier. His face was young but his eyes were a thousand years old, hooded and resigned. I heard the prison superintendent read out his list of crimes, the reason for which he had been sentenced to death, and saw him hear the litany out in unmoved silence. The only thing they could grant him now was his life and that they wouldn't do.

That was an hour ago. Now those hooded eyes are closed forever. I wonder if the people who take his body away realize that I am the man who killed him. I will probably never know the answer. I wonder if I will ever meet them. And what will I say to them if I do?

As I leave the prison complex I look back at the ochre walls. High above is a small black rectangle with some words written on it in English. I don't read English but some years ago one of the warders told me the words written there: 'Central Prison, Poojapura. Opened by His Highness Ravi Vurma on September 23rd, 1886.' Those words meant little to me then: I had heard of His Highness, of course, but that was all.

In the gardens by the road that leads to the gate of the prison compound, past which is the public road, the cashews and the mangoes grow wild. An even, three-foot-high stand of tapioca spreads down the gentle slope, and a bunch of coconut palms stand with their fronds green and gold against the lowering sky. The road curves along the side of the prison wall, the high one with bits of broken glass glinting on top.

A hundred metres from the prison door is a small roundabout manned by a guard in khaki sitting in a sentry box. A right turn at the roundabout takes you to the quarters of the jail staff, blocks of ugly characterless government flats that are nevertheless palaces compared to my own house. To the left is the prison's main gate, the way to freedom.

A breath of wind blows the clouds on and the sun shines through for a moment, and the gardens come alive. The earth is dark and wet and the puddles glisten in the burst of early sunlight. The leaves dance in the breeze and there is the patter of raindrops dripping off leaves on to the soft ground.

We are silent. There are seven of us, most of us of the same clan, I am the aratchar, and the others are my adiyaans. We are like a firing squad, dividing the work amongst us so that the death of the condemned man rests not on any one of us but on all. But as their leader I bear the burden, and they look to me to carry it for them. It is too heavy now.

I hope I will not have to return. Each time I leave, I leave with this thought. Each time I have had to come back in response to the summons from the jail superintendent. This time, though, the thought is much stronger, for this is the first time I have seen the ambulance.

The blackness grows.

I didn't sleep much that night. There were no nightmares, but the memories that came up after I had written just two paragraphs stayed with me. They were sharp, I could see most of the details, but there were pieces missing, names I couldn't remember, and scenes I couldn't see completely. In the morning I had an early breakfast and went to the backyard at eight, pen in hand, and waited impatiently for the words to come, and again they stayed away.

Chellammal came to see what I was doing and found me sitting with my elbows on the desk, my face in my hands, tied to the writing but unable to write a word. 'You've gone mad,' she grumbled. 'You must be ill.'

'Leave me alone,' I told her. 'You accuse me always of wandering about with my friends but now when I sit quietly in the back of the house you grumble at me. What's wrong with you, old woman?' She went away in a huff, her vanity offended. She doesn't like me calling her an old woman. I am, after all, a few years older. But she went, and that was what I wanted.

After she left the words began to flow again. When I stopped, before lunch, I felt drained ... Empty. Empty, and in a sense free.

I noticed only when the passage was finished that my fingers and wrists hurt: I hadn't noticed the pain while writing. It's hard for a man my age to sharpen lost skills and I dreaded the thought of writing again. I had studied only up to the third class at school, and the longest thing I ever wrote was a one-page essay during my last year at school, more than six decades ago.

Each word had come forth like a tonne-weight, but I could see that writing was helping. In the first place, in the middle of the second paragraph, a memory suddenly returned, a memory of the prison gate in the early morning as I looked back at it, a memory of the porch and the dark verandah and the narrow wooden staircase leading to the prison superintendent's office on the first floor. There were memories of the pot-holed road outside, of the lamp-posts along the road to the roundabout, of the man on sentry duty leaning on the lowered beam beyond which lay freedom. And most of all I remembered the intensity with which I wished I would never have to go back. I remembered that clearly, and I remembered one of my adiyaans telling me later that he had never seen me returning so grim-faced from a hanging.

After I had finished the description of my last visit to the prison, I sat and watched the slow sunset with a feeling of lightness. I don't want to lose this lightness, I thought, but even as I slept that night I knew it was slipping away. I came awake restless in the morning. The lightness was gone, and in its place was the urge to write, and the inability.

3

They came on the dot of eleven, as promised, and I was on the doorstep, waiting.

They came in through the gate, silent, and their faces lit up when they saw me. He nodded, and said something that sounded like 'I can see you trouble.' His Tamil was really terrible.

'What?' I asked.

He turned to the woman, and she explained. 'He thinks you're troubled. He sees it in your eyes. He says it's good.' When they spoke together they looked alike, though they were very different, the woman thin and fair and sharp-featured, the man fat and dark and blunt.

'Why does he think my being troubled is good?' I asked.

My irritation must have shown, for there was a placating note in her reply. 'He says you're troubled because you started writing, and it's good that you've started writing.'

'If writing's going to be such a pain,' I snarled, 'then I'm not going to do it. I'll dictate and you sit and write.'

He smiled, 'I told you I can write it for you,' he said haltingly in his bad Tamil. 'You wanted to do it yourself.'

I looked away. His earnestness was amusing. 'I was only pulling your leg,' I said. 'Coffee?'

Again they nodded in unison.

It was hard to talk about what I had written. It was hard to show it to him, like dropping my lungi and exposing myself on a crowded road. While I wondered how to bring up the matter of my writing, he did it for me. 'Did you find time to write a little?'

Time? That was all I had. I wouldn't evade, I decided. 'I wrote a little, and it's not for lack of time that I didn't write more.'

He spoke to the woman then and she said to me, 'Would you like to show us what you've written? It's sometimes difficult, he says, and you might find that it isn't as hard as talking to us.'

He knew. 'Was writing ever as hard for you?' I asked him.

'Yes. I learnt from scratch, just as you're doing now.'

'Oh!' That was a relief. I'd never thought of him as anything other than a writer. 'I'll bring it out for you, then.' Inside the house I picked up the book just as Chellammal stirred sugar into the last of the three cups of coffee.

He handed the book to the woman before sipping his coffee.

She began reading the three pages I'd written. I

felt a twinge of shame at the thought of the mistakes I'd made, of the many ugly black marks on the paper.

As I watched she looked up from the book from time to time and spoke to him in English. She put her finger on the page to indicate where she was, and read it out loud, in Tamil, translating the bits he did not understand. She understood what I'd written, all right: she didn't falter much. When she was through she looked up. 'Is that right?'

'Yes,' I said. I was reassured. It didn't sound bad when she read it out: perhaps it was the way she read it, but there was a rhythm to the passage that I had not noticed when I wrote it.

'How does it sound to you?' she asked the writer in Tamil.

'All right,' he said. He paused, then looked seriously at me. 'It's better than I thought it would be, honestly.'

'I'm glad,' I said. 'Honestly.'

He grinned suddenly.

He dug in his bag and produced two more notebooks. 'Use these, you'll need them.'

Even as I looked at the three notebooks—two in his hand, one in hers—I felt a little stab of fear. 'Do you really expect me to write that much?' I asked.

'No,' he replied. 'You'll write much more. Once it really starts pouring out you won't be able to stop it.'

I blinked at him, unable to imagine filling up all those books. 'And how many years do you think it'll take?' I asked, a trifle sarcastically.

He grinned. 'Up to you. Try it and see.'

'All right … When will you come again?'

'You tell me.'

'In a week?'

'One week from today. Same time. We'll be here.'

~

After they left I took the notebooks back into the house and placed them on the shelf above one of the two folding cots, the one where I kept the clock and a few odd knick-knacks. I marvelled at how easily the two of them had communicated, reading and trying to understand together the private thoughts of a third man, an old man they had no real reason to know. Thinking of the closeness between them, I was reminded of the man with whom I'd been closest.

And so I wrote of my teacher, the one who became my friend.

More than two decades after we last met, I know him the moment I see him.

His name is Prabhakaran. Prabhakaran Maash, which is how they say Master in these parts.

He was a schoolteacher, and had taught me when I was small, when my father could yet afford to send me to school, for in those days schooling was neither compulsory nor cheap. One child's school fees for a month were about the same as a worker's monthly wages. Children learnt what they could at home, and most stayed illiterate, learning to recognize numbers so that they could deal with what little currency they got.

Maash taught me for a couple of years in school. In my boyhood he was awe-inspiring in his black jacket and white turban, with a spotless white mundu wrapped around his legs, his cane in his hand as he went stalking amongst the students, looking for those who had forgotten their homework. The school itself was unimpressive, a long low building divided into rooms, with the headmaster's room at one end. But the masters were impressive. To the students it seemed that they knew everything.

Prabhakaran Maash in particular. His magnificent voice rolled through the little school like a trumpet-burst. It was impossible to sit in his class and not listen to him as he twisted his tongue to get his pronunciation exactly right, to say his words exactly the way the English did. Not that any of us knew that he got nowhere near. We had never heard an Englishman speak. There were few white men in the kingdom of Travancore.

He knew Sanskrit, too, and a little yoga. In his spotless clothes he would do the suryanamaskaar without breathing hard or messing up his clothes. We thought he could do anything. We thought that with his voice and his figure he could rule the world.

So when I see him on the road beside the fields somewhere near Nagercoil at dusk one windy September evening, I know him. He seems to have shrunk since school: he is much smaller, and his new spectacles with their heavy black frames give him an air of even greater scholarship. His hair is as thick as it was at school but it is now more white than grey, and the old crisp turban is gone. The jacket remains, though it is no longer the magnificent immaculate thing it was then: it is greying and mouldy, and there are patches here and there where it has been repaired. His mundu is still the spotless cotton that it used to be, but it is no longer starched and crackling. His walk has lost some of its majesty, and his stride has shortened. He is still lean, but under the jacket is the hint of a swelling waistline. He must be nearing sixty now, and retired.

Maash, like many others, has come upon hard times, but in me he inspires the same awe that he inspired at school. He doesn't know me: how would he, for I was one of the hundreds who passed through his classes.

I do not know whether to approach him. I am troubled and this is the worst time to meet an old acquaintance. We are walking in the same direction, but I slow my pace and fall a few yards further behind him. I follow his regular gait for less than a furlong before he turns and sees me behind him. He beckons me with a nod of the head. 'You look familiar,' he says. 'Did we meet a long time ago? My memory seems to be failing, I am sorry I cannot recognize you.'

Now I cannot avoid it. 'You taught me at school many years ago,' I tell him. 'Nearly thirty years ago. I was one of sixteen boys in your class, and I left school after the third class.'

He shakes his head. 'Thirty years ago? You must have

changed a lot ... You were a small boy then.' He looks at me sideways. 'No, I don't remember.'

'My brothers, one older, one younger, went to the same school.'

'Three boys.' He peers at me, and after a moment his eyes light up behind the spectacles. 'I remember that nose of yours. You must be one of Kamakshinathan Pillai's sons. Which one?'

'Janardhanan,' I reply. 'The one in the middle.'

'Aha!' he says, perking up. 'Not bad for an old man, eh, boy? Where do you live? Somewhere nearby?'

I have been walking for what seems like hours, for my feet hurt. I haven't noticed the time passing because I have been lost in my own world of silence. I look around: the place isn't familiar. Where am I? I take a closer look and I recognize the place. We are not far from my house: only three kilometres, but I rarely come here. 'Yes,' I tell him. 'By the canal, at Peruvilai. A kilometre from Parvathipuram.'

'I too live close by,' he replies. 'Five kilometres away.' With a touch of pride he continues, 'I walk ten to twelve kilometres every day at this time. That's what keeps me fit.'

He does look quite fit for a sixty-year-old man who lives among his books. 'Do you walk this way every day?' I ask. Behind him I see a white egret take off from a field to the east, its wings glowing orange in the sun.

'Not every day, but most days for the past two years or so. I had shifted to Tirunelveli for a while, and when I returned last year I began to walk this route.'

'You must be retired now,' I say to him, 'living quietly.'

A wistful look flashes momentarily in his eyes, then it is gone like the ghost you see from the corner of your eye. 'Quietly?' he says softly. 'I don't know about that ...' He gives himself a little shake. 'And you?' he continues, with a little more vigour. 'And you? What are you doing here? Going somewhere?'

'Out for a walk.'

'Good.' He nods a couple of times, satisfied. 'Do it regularly. But what do you do for a living?'

'I am the aratchar,' I tell him. There is no point in lying to him. 'When we had a king I was the king's hangman, and now I am the government's hangman. I do the job that my father did, and his uncle before him.' He will not speak to me again except to say goodbye, I say to myself, and he will probably change his route to avoid meeting me again.

To my surprise, he doesn't draw away in revulsion. 'You look troubled,' he says, looking at me, concern in his eyes. 'Is something the matter?'

Yes, something is the matter. What it is I do not know. I really do not. 'I can't put it in words,' I tell him.

He starts walking, a little more slowly than before, perhaps, with his head down and his chin on his chest, as he used to when he was deep in thought. After a few minutes he raises his head. 'We can try to find words,' he says. 'Would you like to try? I'll help you as far as I can.'

'Yes,' I tell him. 'Yes. I would like to try ... I've been ...' My voice trails away. In the distance a heron rises with something in its beak.

'Yes? What have you been, boy?' His voice is soft, encouraging. I have never dreamt of Maash having any sympathy for me. I notice that he still calls me boy: I find that both insulting and reassuring.

Then I look at his white hair and sympathetic eyes and the insult vanishes. 'Alone,' I tell him. 'Alone.'

'That we all are,' he says. 'Why do you seem particularly alone?'

'I don't know,' I blurt.

'I can see very clearly that you're shaken,' he says. 'Perhaps you need to think a little more before you talk about it. Would you like to come this way tomorrow at the same time, and try to talk? I'll be here.'

'Yes,' I tell him. 'Thanks.'

'Thanks for what?'

'The others ... The others don't talk. They shut me out of their lives.'

'They don't know, that's why. Leave them be.'

'Yes.'

'And be here tomorrow. Let me wish you good evening, it's time for me to turn back.'

I nod. He starts briskly back the way he came, his black jacket fading slowly in the gathering dark, his white mundu gleaming palely as it flaps about his legs in the breeze.

I started on this after the writer had left. I sat with it through that afternoon, and the next morning. When Chellammal called me in for lunch the next afternoon, it was nearly done. I told her to wait a few minutes while I finished off the paragraph but it took me half an hour, and when I did go in the rice gruel and the beans were cooling in their pots. She grumbled throughout the meal but for once I didn't really hear her because I was enjoying the meal, cold though it was.

The words were beginning to come on their own, and with them came more memories of Maash.

In the days that followed that meeting by the fields, I met him several times. In the beginning it was like going back to school. He was still a sort of demigod figure, and I found myself hesitating to speak to him. It took me two more meetings before I was able to tell him why I had been so visibly upset the evening we first met, and even that only after he told me about his own weaknesses.

The writer would be back in six days. In those six days I would write a lot more. I knew it would happen, there was a thickness in my chest that told of words waiting to emerge. Words about Maash.

The third time we meet I find him a little before the spot that we met the first two times. This time he explains his route to me in great detail, and the approximate time he reaches each landmark. 'I'm telling you all this,' he says, 'so that you'll know where to catch me. If there's a lot you want to say, catch me early. If there isn't much, later on will do. As long as you don't mind walking along with me, which I don't think you do.'

'I don't mind,' I tell him. 'But would you like to come to my house?'

He looks at me out of his black eyes, hiding his feelings. 'Perhaps I will someday,' he says, 'but for the time being it is better we meet here.' We walk on in silence for a furlong or so, and he turns to me. 'You must be wondering why I don't invite you to my house, where we can talk in the daytime. You know that I have nothing much to do since I retired.'

I nod.

'Well,' he continues, 'it's not something that I've told anyone else. You're the only one who knows this, and we'll keep it that way.' His voice drops to something only a little more than a whisper. 'My wife, she's got rather fixed ideas of what's proper and what's not.'

Just like Chellammal, I think, just like the women in any family. They have fixed ideas about timings and food and how children are to be brought up and so on. 'I understand,' I say, without really understanding why he's saying this.

'Also about people.'

Again, just like Chellammal. She won't allow some of the men I know into the house. We have quarrelled over this many times in the decades of our marriage but haven't ever really settled the issue. 'Yes,' I say.

'And about castes.'

There it is. Maash is a Brahmin, or something close. He belongs to a caste unimaginably above mine. 'I understand,' I repeat.

'You don't,' he says, with intensity. 'You don't understand.'

'What don't I understand?' I ask, puzzled.

'Can't you see,' he says, 'that she nags me? She won't let me live in peace. Do you think I need to walk twelve kilometres each day to keep fit? Half that distance would do. I walk so much for an extra hour of quiet. To be without her wretched voice screaming in my ear. If I took you home she might let you in but my life for two months after would be torture.'

My omniscient demigod is really only a henpecked husband.

The second passage about Maash was done in a couple of hours. When I looked up from the book my fingers and my wrist were hurting, as were my ankles, for I had been sitting cross-legged all that time. The sun was much lower, I noticed, and there was a strong breeze that scattered the dry leaves lying on the ground and threatened to blow my notebook away. I was thirsty, tired and very, very light in my heart, and I couldn't get my mind off Maash even as I stretched and picked up the table and the books to put them safely inside the house.

I never forgot the amazement I had felt when I heard that Maash couldn't control his wife's temper. At school he had been very powerful, very authoritative. We had thought he could rule the world.

I followed him to his house once, just to get a glimpse of this woman who could dominate my old idol. She turned out to be thin and bleak-eyed, dressed in the conventional nine-yard sari of the upper castes, with a voice that would have done justice to a peacock. I saw her jutting chin and wondered how Maash could have been misguided enough to marry this woman.

I couldn't help thinking then that perhaps I wasn't so badly off, after all. Nobody could drive me out of my home, and when I spoke firmly my wife listened to me.

When we meet for the fourth time I catch him early. The sun is in the sky and there is a lingering warmth that can still bring sweat. At this time Maash is only a kilometre or two into his walk, still fresh, with the evening before him.

I have prepared for this meeting. I have to steel myself to talk, though he has told me at least four times that I must learn to treat him as an equal. It was only on the third meeting that I began to understand that he, too, was human. Even so ... He must have known. He must have known how I felt about him, and he would have struggled to tell me that he was henpecked. He would have struggled to find the courage to tell me something that would knock him off the pedestal that he knew I had placed him on.

I feel a swell of pride that he has chosen me of all people for his confidant. I wonder why. I will ask him today.

I wait in the shade of a tree by a bus-stop for him to come. It is five o'clock, and there are many vehicles on the road, buses and trucks and bullock carts and a few cars. In 1961, nearly fifteen years after Independence, life is very different from what it used to be in the days of the king and the British.

I see him turn a corner half a furlong away. His walk is distinctive, and vigorous. He looks younger than his years, and I wonder why his wife treats him badly. She should consider herself lucky to be married to a man like that.

He sees me and smiles. There is something in his eyes I can't fathom, a sort of distance. I fall in step beside him as he draws up. 'Good evening,' he says. 'You look as if you intend to talk a long while today.'

'Yes,' I tell him. 'That's why I'm here early.'

'Not only that. You have a very determined look. As if you have unpleasant things to tell me.'

'I don't know about the unpleasantness … I just want to talk of parts of my life that no one knows about.'

'Go ahead. But let's get away from here, to some place less crowded.' We walk away from the racket of cycle bells and car horns and peddlers.

Some ten minutes later we reach a quiet road by the fields. Maash still has some of his old authority about him; people tend to keep their distance from him. 'Yes,' he says when he thinks we can talk. 'What got you so upset when we met here last week?'

'I had just returned from a hanging. From three hangings in three days.'

'Does it make a difference to you?'

How can I explain? How can I explain that my mind

goes foggy for a few days after each hanging? How can I explain that to proceed with another hanging during the fog is the hardest thing I have ever done in my life, and I was forced to do it twice?

'It does,' I say. 'It makes a big difference.'

He looks at me closely. 'What happens? Do you go into a shock after a killing? Do you find everything a little hazy, as if you're seeing it from far away, and without any real control over what's happening?'

He seems to understand the fog. 'Yes. Something like that.'

'And when you did three in three days you found it very much worse than usual?'

That wasn't all there was to it. 'My wife was pregnant when I left. When I returned, I found she had delivered a daughter.'

'So what?' he says. 'You don't have anything against daughters, do you?'

In a way I suppose I do. Daughters are hard to raise, and harder still to marry off. They are more vulnerable to trouble than boys. But having a daughter wouldn't add to my shock. A child is a child, after all. 'No,' I say. 'That's got nothing to do with it.'

'What is it, then?'

'I don't know.'

'Tell me what happened. Slowly.'

'Nothing. I went to Trivandrum, I did those hangings, and when I came back I found my wife suckling this new baby. I saw the baby and … and I found I couldn't touch her.'

'You have something against the child?'

'How can I? She's only a baby.'

'Then why can't you touch her?'

The answer comes, in a flash. I blurt it out instantly. 'Because she might be one of my victims.'

He stops and turns and places his right hand on my shoulder. 'So what?' he asks. 'She's your daughter. Even if she had a life before this one she wouldn't know about it, and neither will you. It doesn't matter. Just look after her like your other daughters. That's if you believe in rebirth and so on, which I personally don't.'

It makes sense, what he's saying. 'I've always been confused about god and rebirth and lives and so on,' I say slowly.

'What is the need for confusion?' he asks. 'Does it matter whether there is a god or not, or whether there is rebirth or not? Just do your duty, the rest will take care of itself. What else is dharma all about?'

The morning after I wrote this, I felt I was stretching myself out too long. There was a weariness that comes from sitting too long and doing nothing. I went for a long walk, like Maash, to get my blood warmed up before sitting down to write.

Along the way I met Murugan of the coffee shop. 'What's happened?' he asked when I sat on the bench under the awning in front of his stall. 'You look happy.'

That was true. What I'd written these past few days had left me light. Was it the writing, or just the fact that I was thinking about something long enough to make it clear in my own mind? I didn't know. But as I sat there sipping Murugan's sweet milky tea my mind went back to Maash.

He was so sure of himself in these matters. When he told me about doing my duty, I remember, I wanted to ask him, who decides what my duty is and what it is not? Who is to tell me what is good and what is not?

There was much there that disturbed me. Until then I had thought that whatever the government did was good … I believed in the government as I had believed earlier that the king of Travancore was god come down to earth. But no longer. I was young then, not much past forty, and the future ahead disturbed me.

And it had become clear to me that Maash too had his limitations. For all his learning and his book knowledge, he couldn't run his home as a man should. He spoke of duty, but wasn't it his duty to quell his wife when she started screaming at him? Why hadn't he taken her back to her parents' house when he found out her nature? So when he talked of my duty, did he really know what he was saying?

I remember the frustration and discomfort of wanting to ask him all those questions and having to hold them back, for at the time I was confused, and I did not feel I had the words.

There is much today I could ask him about dharma, but he is gone now.

4

Dharma. I took it for granted always. In the days of the king your dharma was simple: to do as the king told you to.

That was a mistake. The king worked for himself, not for his people, that was clear. The king was human, like anyone else, like Maash or myself. Often a selfish man—I think you have to be to be a king. You have to be even more selfish to make up a legend that makes you god's representative on earth; this is what the king of Travancore did, some centuries ago. Maash told me that this is what other kings all over the world have done over the centuries. No wonder the kings didn't want us to think independently.

Sitting outside with the notebook in the warm afternoon breeze, with a light sweat on my bare chest and the dog sleeping by my side, I remembered something I'd seen long ago … I didn't even know whether I'd seen it, or only heard it described by my father, Kamakshinathan. I wondered for a while whether to put it down in the notebook, then realized that if the writer didn't want it he could always cut it out.

This whole section was very hard to write since it violated some of my earliest ideals, the principles that we were taught in childhood. It felt like treason. This is why they take such pains to teach us in childhood: to make it hard for us to put away those teachings later. Obey, they say when you are a child. Obey your parents. Obey the king. Obey the government. Obey your elders. Obey your superiors at work. I always obeyed, and look where it got me!

My hands trembled when I started to write. But here I spoke from the heart. If what I said was treason, so be it. If my memory was at fault, so be it.

~

What was good for the king was good for his kingdom. Everyone believed this principle, from the king himself down to the meanest citizen. The citizens venerated the king so much that they didn't refer to him by name: they referred to him by the star under which he was born, for they thought he was their god on earth. Even I thought so at one time. Only the British didn't think so, but they took care not to tell the king that. They took care not to tell anyone, especially not the common people.

This was in the days before the British left India to her own destiny. Then I was not a citizen of India. I belonged to the princely state of Travancore, which was, in those days, a semi-independent attachment to

British India. It was semi-independent because the king was only *seen* to rule: in truth, his diwan and the white political resident handled the reins between them. But they, too, maintained the charade of the divine right of the king: Marthanda Varma, of the two-thousand-year-old royal dynasty, dedicated his kingdom in the eighteenth century to Lord Padmanabha, and it suited them to stick to the old order.

Obey, they said, and the citizens obeyed.

The king was no god but a man, a lot wealthier than you or me, but a man all the same. He was just as close to god, or distant from him, as you or me. There was proof of this distance. If the king was the earthly face of god, why would he need absolution for anything? Yet he needed it. He proclaimed it. The hangman knew.

The idea must have come from the king's many sycophants. His court was full of them. One of his courtiers must have suggested it: the king must be protected from the guilt of killing a citizen. And of course the king thought it was a good idea.

As a youth I wondered why they bothered so much about the king. His soldiers caught the man. His judge sentenced the fellow. I killed him with the help of the officials in the prison. So why was the king at the centre of the rituals? How was he involved?

Father told me this when I was young, and later I saw it for myself. Every death warrant—these days they call it the black warrant—said that the sentence must be ratified by the king. When the judge passed the sentence, the date for the condemned man's execution was fixed, and following routine the court sent a mercy petition to the king. At the palace the officials made sure that the king got the petition only late in the afternoon of the day before the execution. The king, when he got the petition, invariably commuted the condemned man's sentence to life imprisonment.

This was an enormous joke, and to help you understand it, I must first give you a little history of time. In the old days, before these newfangled measurements, before all these clocks and watches became so common, our day was measured by the sun. A day began at sunrise and ended at the next sunrise. In the horoscopes made then, if you were born by day your time of birth would be so many nazhikas and so many vinazhikas after sunrise. If you were born at night your time of birth would be written as so many nazhikas and vinazhikas before sunrise. (If, that is, you could afford to have an astrologer do these things for you. In those days it was only for the rich: no one ever drew up my horoscope because nobody noted down the time when I was born ... I don't even know the day, far less the hour and the minute when I was born.)

When the judge sentenced a man to death—women were never sentenced to death, they were exiled—he also put down the date on which the condemned man was to be executed. The king's men, in the name of humanity and the law, tried to give the prisoner as long a life as possible within the limits of the sentence. And thus arose the practice of execution at dawn. The king's men would execute their victim at the last possible moment before the end of the appointed day: just before sunrise. The law said that the man must be declared dead before sunrise, so the ritual of hanging began at about four in the morning.

The king's messenger, the one carrying the reprieve, would set out from the palace at the crack of dawn, and invariably reach the prison just after the execution. He would arrive in time to see the body being brought up from the pit beneath the scaffold, and the farce would begin.

'Oh my god!' the messenger would exclaim. 'You've killed the prisoner already!'

'Yes, he's dead,' the prison superintendent would reply, producing his papers, signed by the judge. 'See, I have the sentence here. I've done what I was told to do, at the time I was told to do it.'

The messenger would bow and present his own papers, signed by the king. 'But I have a reprieve for him. The king signed it at dusk yesterday, and as you know we do not work after sunset or before sunrise.'

'Ah! What a pity! It's come too late for this one.' The superintendent would shake his head sadly and move on.

'Why did you hurry with the hanging?' the messenger would say, rushing after him.

'I didn't hurry, I kept him alive as long as I could.' The superintendent would shuffle the papers in his hand. 'Here is the date ... See? I just followed instructions from the court. Why didn't you come earlier?'

'I have rules to follow, just like you. I shouldn't work after sunset or before sunrise. Well, this is Lord

Padmanabha's kingdom, and He has made the rules. Let it be on His head, then, the weight of this killing.'

The messenger would return to the palace and his other duties, and the superintendent to his own. Each returned secure in the knowledge that he had done what was needed of him. The warders would go back to their job of beating the prisoners. The king would sleep the sleep of the just. Lord Padmanabha, of course, wouldn't deign to tell anyone what he thought of the whole thing. Sometimes the messenger would arrive early, perhaps because he was eager to see the hanging. He would wait, impatient and fidgeting, until the whole thing was over. Only then would he deliver his papers and play out the farce with the superintendent.

And only the hangman would go home with blood on his hands and a life on his conscience.

It didn't matter in the old days, because the hangman really was the king's hatchet man. In the old days—maybe two hundred years ago—the hangman came from a family of handpicked men, loyal to the death, willing to obey the king's most ridiculous command without question. Those men were close to the king, and this made them arrogant. They killed without compunction, and one life more or less didn't matter to them.

But I was no hatchet man. Every life mattered to me. I am of peasant blood, of a family of farmers and tillers of the land, taught over generations to nurture life rather than to take it. Destiny placed me beside the scaffold. The king's conscience was eased, the officials were just doing their job, and the messenger ... well, the messenger didn't care either. But the hangman cared. Strange, isn't it, that the rituals took care of the king and the messengers and the superintendent, but ignored the hangman, the only one who cared?

~

The king was my master until Independence, and to speak against him goes against my grain, but I have done it. I had no choice, really, for I don't want anyone else to be damned as I have been. I have borne the guilt too long. If what I have written is treason, let them do what they will. I have nothing left that they can take.

I started about the king late one afternoon, and stopped for the day after one paragraph in which I made at least fifty mistakes. I sat there until the sun went low and it was too dark for my old eyes to see what I had written. Next morning I woke with a heaviness. I think it came from not writing what I had wanted to.

In the morning I struggled again. The memory of that awful arrogance drove me on. A fragment of memory emerged, of Maash talking of the king, many years after our reunion on the road.

Maash feels much as I do about the king. I discover the depth of Maash's contempt for the old king and for the government on an evening when we cannot walk far because he has sprained an ankle.

'Sometimes I miss the days of the king,' I say to him as he hobbles along and I walk slowly by his side. He has just celebrated his 72nd year, and is cheerful despite the injury. 'Life was simpler then: the king told me what to do, and I did it.'

'The king was a traitor,' Maash replies. In old age his voice has weakened a little, but it is still strong. His tone is harsh and bitter, and his mouth goes awry with distaste, as if he doesn't like to speak of the king. 'The royal family were willing to do anything to keep their throne. In many ways they were worse than the British.'

'How can you say that about a dynasty that has occupied the throne for over two thousand years?' Maash sometimes gets things mixed up, as old people often do, and I feel that he's mixed up our king with some other.

Maash's face stays bitter, his voice harsh. 'What matters is not how long they ruled but how well they ruled.'

'Didn't they rule well? I don't know.'

'Exactly. They brainwash you.'

'Brainwash?' It is a new word to me. 'What's that?'

'They make you believe what they want you to believe.'

'Who's they?' I ask, puzzled.

'They? The king. The government. The British.'

'I don't understand.'

His face twists again, in anger. 'I'm sure you don't,' he says. 'Do you know that the king was an ally of the British?'

'No,' I reply slowly. 'I have heard that the British treated the king as an equal.'

'Nonsense. The king was a vassal. Do you know that there used to be a Britisher in the king's court called the political resident?'

'No. Who was he?'

'He was the British king's man. The king of Travancore bowed to him.'

'But Marthanda Varma made Travancore.'

'Yes, he did. He defeated the Dutch at Colachel, too. But do you know what advice he gave his nephew from his deathbed? Stay friends with the British—that was his parting advice. And every king who followed Marthanda Varma did just that. They sold their independence to the British just to keep power over the citizenry in their own hands.'

'That's true, but …' I don't know what to say.

'You yourself told me about that ridiculous custom at the hangings, of having a messenger deliver the reprieve just too late for it to be of any use. Do you remember telling me?'

'Yes, I do.' I had told him about it the second or third time I met him.

'Do you see how selfish it is? He takes care of himself and a few picked servants and to hell with the rest of the people. Do you think the kings were any better than the whites?'

Come to think of it, they weren't. They took care of their own picked few, as did the whites, leaving us poor people to suffer. There wasn't any difference really between the white rule and the king's.

~

Thinking of these matters, of kings and foreigners, made me sad and pensive. Writing of this kind re-awakened old anger. In a way it was good, for it took me back to the days of my youth. I wrote some of this with the fire of my youth still in me, but it didn't sound good. I tore the sheets out of the notebook and threw them away and started all over again, and found more anger.

Before each hanging, I go to the hangman's temple at Bimaneri.

That, too, is a Bhadrakali temple, like Ramayyan's which is nearby, but much more elaborate. And there is a sword there that was presented to the original family of hangmen when they earned the right to execute the king's enemies some two hundred years ago.

I believe the original grant that the hangman's family received was of some sixty acres of what used to be called karamozhivu—tax-free land. The land was solely the owner's, and the king took no revenue from him. This aside, there was more land—fields of paddy, called nelam. And there was uncultivated land, on which cashews grew wild, called porayidam. Along with the grant of land came money: seventeen rupees a month, I think. Considering that this was more than Maash's salary nearly two centuries later, it must have been a small fortune in those days, especially since all the food that the family needed came from the land.

The British reviewed this grant sometime early in the 19th century, they say, when Colonel Munro was the resident. It was probably increased, for the hangman was an important part of the law of those days.

So the clan grew rich. By degrees they became janmis, landed gentry. They had wealth and servants, and every now and again they got a message directly from the king, so regardless of their caste, which was not the highest, they had the grudging respect of everyone in the area.

But when it came to marrying off the women in their family it was a different matter altogether. In the first place, since the clan followed the matrilineal system, the right was inherited not by the son of the hangman but his son-in-law, the husband of his eldest daughter, who was usually his sister's son. If she remained unmarried, it went to the husband of the second daughter, and so on. So the hangman's daughters remained unwed, and a girl in the family was even more of a burden than she was in other families in the area.

So the family began to look for someone who would do the hangman's job for them. It was the ideal solution—the family would no longer carry the taint of being professional killers, and yet keep the wealth they had been given for being the king's official executioners.

They found my father. He was a distant cousin of theirs, close enough to be given the job. He took it because he must have known hunger, and one of the perks of the job was a grant of three large sacks of paddy, each about 85 kilograms, from each of the two annual harvests. From this we got about 300 kilos of rice every year—we had to husk it ourselves—which was enough for a large family. It was more than enough for the five of us—Father, Mother, and the three children—even though we occasionally had others living with us. There was a little left over that we could exchange for some cloth; for a mundu and a loincloth for the boys every year; and for oil and salt and spices and other everyday needs. This, supplemented with the allowance Father got for each hanging, saw us through the worst years. But there was never quite enough.

The family, my father's cousins, kept the acres of land, and they kept the sword in the temple at Bimaneri, giving us, grudgingly, the patch of land on which we built a house. It was a small one-room house by the fields where we all lived. Father did the dirty work for them for a pittance, and I continue to do it for the same pittance. It is a matter of survival, so I do it. It is not fair, and sometimes the resentment burns in me, but when I see that my children are fed it doesn't burn so much.

The resentment burns at its fiercest when I see that family looking down their noses at us. They point at us in proof that they are not the family of hangmen. They treat us with the contempt with which they treat any menial. And all the while they enjoy the fruit of the hangman's position.

Before I started on this I saw the torn discarded sheets lying crumpled and forlorn on the ground. I retrieved them quickly, before the wind took them: the writer had said, don't throw away anything you write, and I was obeying him. Despite my age and experience, obedience still comes naturally to me, I think. I was lucky the pages were still there: sometimes the dog picks up small things and chews them up for his own entertainment. I flattened the sheets out, wiped the dirt off them, then pinned them on to the last page of the book and left them there for the writer.

5

The next morning I went for a walk again, in search of new memories.

The summer came early and the sun was too harsh. The wells were drying up. The birds had come out early, as had the snakes, driven by hunger. In the distance a tractor was ploughing dry fields, dragging hard iron teeth through the dun soil.

I stood watching the tractor and the busy herons following it, and my mind began to wander. It's one of the troubles that comes with old age. Perhaps if I could talk to someone it would help bring back dim images from my past. But I only had Chellammal, and I have shared so little with her that it seemed pointless to start now. How would I begin? But thinking of it I found something to write about: Silence.

I have never opened my heart completely to anyone, not even to Maash. I remember, people used to stop talking when I passed by. Even now they do it, even those who know me.

I suppose it comes with the job. It's much better these days, thanks perhaps to writers like my friend with the beard, but in the old days it was terrible. When I returned from a hanging they would look away. I would see the shutters come down over their eyes and they would turn away and make inconsequential small talk for a few days. When I moved off I often thought I could hear them whispering about me: There goes the hangman, just back from a hanging.

In a way I think I hold it against them. I shouldn't, but I do. I was doing something that the government, or the king, asked me to do. Ordered me to do. How could I not obey?

It wasn't easy to do. After each hanging I would have liked to come back to a gentle welcome at home and elsewhere, but I never had one. Chellammal, of course, left me alone for a few days after I returned; in any case, I couldn't open out to her. The others … They were my friends. They knew that I was vulnerable when I returned, and yet they kept their distance from me when I most needed their help.

The only good thing that came of it was that Velu at the coffee shop never refused me credit. Murugan, his son, has been the same, so I've never lacked for a cup of tea or a snack during the day. But even Velu and Murugan, who trusted me with their money, wouldn't trust me with their words.

The silence is permanent. Relatives outside my

immediate family don't speak to me even now. And they prefer, as far as possible, not to talk about me. I have a distant relative, a sort of cousin, who lives nearby, close to the temple at Suchindram. He worked at the temple for many years and is now retired. He lives in some dignity in a narrow dark house that overlooks the pond of dirty water outside the temple. He discourages people from trying to find me. Another writer, one who worked for a newspaper, met him a year ago while trying to trace me.

'What do you want to know about the hangman?' my relative asked the reporter. 'Why do you want to find out about him? He dealt with criminals at one time, and now that time is over. Why don't you write about that temple in front of you? It is still alive. Thousands of people come every month to see it.'

'But my chief asked me to write about the hangman,' the reporter insisted.

'Well, you can say that the family was appointed by Marthanda Varma,' replied my relative. 'They were given land and a grant of seventeen rupees a month, which was a fortune in those days. But the family has now gone to the dogs. They do no hangings, and the last hangman's sons survive on manual labour when they can find any. That's all you need to know. I don't see why you should want to meet him.'

The reporter eventually found me, through another reporter. He came and then was in a hurry to leave. He had heard of the hangman and had come expecting something more than this humble little house by the fields. Perhaps he expected to see some wealth or grandeur, not knowing that I was not part of the original aratchar family. He asked me about the rituals of hanging and left. Before he left, he told me everything that my distant relative had told him.

All of it was nonsense. The family that got a fortune from the kings is not mine. I did the job they should have done, and I did it to the best of my ability. I have nothing to be ashamed of. All my children are literate, even my daughters. My daughters are all married, though it was hard to find someone willing to marry into a hangman's family. My sons are all employed, and the youngest has a government job: he is a mechanic with one of the state's transport corporations. I have done what I could for my children.

I have failed or succeeded in life as much as any other man. I have done my best. Yet no one wants to get too close to the hangman. It's as if the man is a leper …

I bring silence wherever I go.

In the prison, on the day before a hanging, the prison guards are silent. There is none of the bickering and the small talk that is part of any normal group of working men. Instead, there is a heavy silence.

The other prisoners know that there will be a hanging on such and such a day: no hanging is a secret. Prisoners sentenced to death spend their time until death or reprieve in a cell that is one of six, in a row reserved for condemned men: this row, death row, is called the condemned cell. After all legal processes are over, when a sentence is confirmed and all appeals have failed, the warders put a board on the door of the cell, announcing that so and so will be executed on such and such day. And on that day and the day before it, the day when I arrive, all through the prison there is a silence.

In the daytime when the convicts work there is silence always, but when they return from the fields or the gardens or workshops where they have been assigned, there is always the sound that must arise when several hundred men are together. There are prayers in the church or the mosque near the prison hospital. There are chants from the temple next to the tower that rises like a stubby three-storied phallus from the centre of the prison complex. There is the buzz of conversation and occasionally some laughter.

But after I arrive all that ends. Only the bell atop the tower breaks the silence with its quarter-hourly single ring and the long ring at a quarter-to-six, when the guards count the prisoners before locking them into their cells for the night. At dusk there is birdsong as the birds come to their nests in the trees around the prison wall: they sing and quarrel as always, for they don't care that a man will die. And why should they? Does a man care when he kills a bird?

In the prison portico, facing the stone with Ravi Varma's name on it, is the deputy jailer's office where I report as soon as I come in. There are certain formalities to be gone through, details to be recorded. The warders take care of all that: it's their job, maintaining records, and I have no part in it. They smile weakly at me when they see me, but they don't speak to me unless they have to. I see a couple of prison guards in uniform getting ready to go off duty. They lounge around, watching me. These men are not of the police force, the marks on their shoulders are different. The police have KP, for Kerala Police, written on their epaulettes, these men have KJ, for Kerala Jail, written there.

I've seen half-a-dozen of these deputy warders ... Their names and faces blur in my mind, and I remember only their uniforms. Uniforms with three stars on the epaulettes.

As soon as I arrive there begins a flurry of silent activity. Part of my job is to test the gallows. When I reach the prison in the afternoon, the prison superintendent himself greets me. He tells me the name of the man I am to hang, and his weight, so that I can calculate the length of the drop required to kill him without seriously damaging him. The superintendent tries to get to know me, he asks me questions about myself, about my wife and my children and my house, and he tells me if any bigwigs are coming to see my work. But not the others. They keep their distance, unless there is work to be done.

And work there is. The scaffold must be clean. It must be washed and readied for the execution. In the old days, when it was used often—almost every week—there was no need to clean it. But now, after the time of the king, when there are only four or five executions a year, the cobwebs come up.

The timber is black with age, rich teak that came from the Maharaja's own forests, they say. But then all forests in the kingdom were the Maharaja's own at one time ... My mind wanders sometimes. Age brings its weaknesses and its consolations. I cannot dwell on anything, even on the lives I have taken. Where were we? Ah, silence.

They tell me there is silence in the prison *after* a hanging as well, among guards and prisoners. Why are they silent? Do they mourn the dead man? A criminal convicted by the court?

The warders are silent as we work. The scaffold itself consists of two uprights some six feet apart, with a rectangular trapdoor in between and a crosspiece across the top. It must be cleaned. The big cylindrical stone weight with the carved handle must be brought out of the storeroom where they keep it when it's not in use, for me to test the rope. The trapdoor on which the condemned man stands is hinged at one end and held in place at the other by two tongues of steel. A detachable lever sticking out of the wooden floor right next to one of the uprights pulls back these tongues, and the trapdoor opens downwards. The lever is kept in the storeroom: this, too, has to be brought out, and the mechanism oiled if it has rusted. At least three ropes must be available, they are brought from the stores along with the lever and the stone weight and a container of oil.

Everything must proceed smoothly. There are others to help, four or five youngsters under my direction and prison staff to get us whatever we need. The youngest and lightest of the adiyaans climbs up the eastern pillar of the scaffold to pass the first of the ropes over the top of the crosspiece. There are three footrests, each sticking two inches out of the pillar, and he has to step carefully, resting his weight on his toes to prevent himself from falling on to the trapdoor. To the side of the same pillar is the little hook to which the free end of the rope is tied, the hook on which the following day the weight of a man will rest. One of the guards picks up the lever and dusts it off before fixing it in its slot. Three adiyaans and a guard struggle with the stone dummy with which we will test the rope.

In the old days the testing was entirely the aratchar's responsibility. I don't know of any aratchar whose rope broke on the day of the hanging: I wonder as I watch what would have happened in the days of Marthanda Varma if an aratchar failed to test his rope properly and it broke.

I prepare the noose. This is a simple knot, one that I have tied many times. I could do it blindfolded, but I take great care over it, for if anything goes wrong it is my responsibility. When the knot is done, I thread it around the neck of the stone weight. This weight is interesting, it was carved for the purpose at the orders of the king in the early nineteenth century. It's a cylinder with slots in which more carved stones can be added to increase the weight. The new rules, the ones they introduced in 1958, say that we should test the scaffold with at least one-and-a-half times the weight of the condemned man, but in the old days we used to test it with approximately 150 kilograms; more than one-and-a-half times the weight of any of the men I've hanged. That's a strange thought: most of the men I've executed have been in bad shape. Perhaps it's the prison diet.

But then condemned men are confined to the condemned cell, and they do no work. All they do is eat and drink and sleep ... Perhaps they don't sleep. Perhaps they face themselves every waking moment, face the enormity of their crimes ... I don't know. I wouldn't like to exchange places with one of them.

At last we are ready to test the scaffold. The ropes are ready, all three of them, the lever is in place, and the trapdoor hinges have been checked.

We do it first without the weight. The lever moves easily now, freshly oiled, the steel tongues holding up the trapdoor sliding smoothly. When my senior adiyaan, Kumaran, jerks the lever, the trapdoor drops open with a muffled thud: it swings downwards and strikes one of the uprights, which extends underneath the platform on which the trapdoor is fixed. The point where it strikes the upright is padded with half an inch of sacking to prevent a loud noise, and a blunt hook fixed to the wall to catch the end of the trapdoor prevents it from bouncing off the upright and hitting the body as it hangs at the end of the rope.

I go down into the well below the scaffold, the dark pit where the body will hang for at least fifteen minutes after the hanging. The end of the rope is almost exactly at the level of the platform above.

In the pit I undo the catch to free the end of the

door so that it can be swung back upwards into position to test the next rope. The lever always squeaks mightily when I try it the first time, for it is months since it has been used and I can see the rust forming on the metal. Another adiyaan uses a pole to lift the free end of the trapdoor back into position: he has done it before and can do it easily even in the dark of the well.

We do another run, this time with the weight. The stone is heavy and takes three of us to move it on to the trapdoor, which creaks loudly when it bears the combined weight of the stone and the three people manoeuvring it into position. But we know that the trapdoor is solid teak ribbed with metal and the creaks are just a mild protest. There is a faint sheen of sweat on the adiyaans' chests from working in the warmth of the afternoon sun, and they breathe heavily.

This time the lever is harder to pull, with the weight of the stone sitting on the trapdoor pushing the tongues down. The adiyaan has to jerk the lever sharply to get it moving, and it moves suddenly. This time the thump is louder and more abrupt, as we watch the weight disappear. Where the stone had been, we now see the rope swinging gently ... It stops swinging in seconds; with a man at the end of it the rope would continue to swing for much longer. Again I descend into the well to inspect the uprights.

We do this twice more. Then it is time to go. The guards and the deputy jailer who have helped us accompany us to the gate. 'Four tomorrow morning,' the deputy jailer says.

'Yes,' I nod at him. I am sweating, not just because of the labour or the windless afternoon's warmth but from something more. On the way we see a couple of prisoners going about their business. They avoid looking at us, and the guards avoid looking at them. The prisoners know that one of their number will die the next morning, and the knowledge hovers darkly in their eyes.

Each time I use it, I see how well they designed the scaffold. Everything is in place. Everything is designed so that the hanging goes smoothly.

When I go back to the guest house that night I ask myself: Why do we spend so much of our lives making death smoother than life?

~

After I finished this passage in the evening, I hadn't the strength to go on my usual rounds of the coffee shop, or the enthusiasm … I didn't want to fall into the rut again, the rut I had been in for the past quarter-century.

I was too tired. Enough, I thought, enough for the week. The next day my daughter-in-law from Calicut would be here with her two children, my grandchildren. They are better off than we are, and they have a bigger house, with a black-and-white television set. I don't know how comfortable they are here: they never stay long. Chellammal is happy when they come, for there is company, and help in the kitchen, and I get time with my grandsons.

I would leave writing alone for a few days.

6

But I was restless throughout the following day. The grandchildren arrived with their mother but my mind was on the book. Writing brought me no comfort, and yet there was a sense of despair when I wasn't putting down words on paper.

The writer came, this time without the woman. I wanted to talk to him, tell him about the blackness that seemed to fill my mind sometimes. There was an undercurrent of urgency that was driving me on, not just the pleasure and relief of writing. I didn't know why, but I wanted to finish this writing as soon as I could.

'It's hard to be patient,' I said to him and hoped he would understand.

We were drinking coffee. He finished his in one last big gulp and said, 'You spoke of going for walks with Maash … Would you like to go for a walk now?'

'Right now?' I asked, surprised.

'Yes, now,' he replied, and added, 'and don't worry, I understand what you say, I've been working on my Tamil. Hasn't it improved?'

It had. 'But what about all this I've written?'

He looked at the pages. 'There's quite a bit here. I'll take it with me. I'll need my friend to help me with this, just in case I miss something.'

He rose, ready for the walk. The road outside my house is not tarred, it is beaten earth that turns into slush during the rains. In summer it is hard and dusty, and the wind raises brown clouds that settle on our clothes. Each footfall raises a tiny cloud. 'Your clothes will gather dirt,' I told him.

'I don't mind,' he said.

We walked through the fields, where it was quiet. The paddy ran along the path, at a lower level, so that water could flow into it. All around were traces of the old system of irrigation, tanks called eris, and I pointed them out to him as we went off the path on to the embankments that separated the fields. 'Is this where you grew up?' he asked.

'Yes, my father's house was right next to our present house. It collapsed in the rains many years ago.'

'Tell me about your childhood. How many of you were there?'

'Three of us, all male. I was the one in the middle. My elder brother's name was Raman, and my younger brother's is Paraman. Father's name was Kamakshinathan …'

'What was your childhood like?' he asked.

A little ahead of us, a small boy wearing only shorts

stepped up to a shopkeeper and held up a hand with a few coins in it. I heard him ask in a high voice for a little kerosene, which the shopkeeper gave him in a tiny plastic bag. Then the boy was off, running homewards with the night's supply of oil in his hands. I stopped on the dusty road. An image had come to my mind, full-blown.

He seemed to understand. 'Let's go back. Put it down on paper before you lose it. I'll see you tomorrow.'

We went back quickly and silently, by the shortest route, and when we got there he left without fuss. I pulled the table out into the late afternoon sun and began to write.

~

To a child any house is sufficient.

The one-room thatch house is sufficient. There is room to sleep, to shelter from the sun when it is too hot, and to cook and eat. There is even room to play, if I feel like it, but Mother doesn't let us play in the house. She drives us out into the yard for that.

There are trees in the yard, a mango and a jack, with two coconut palms in a corner. There is a neem tree, robust, with a thick trunk and many branches that I have climbed. In summer the mango and the jack bear fruit. Then there is enough to eat, a change from the rice gruel that is the staple food for most of the year. The neem gives us much: twigs for toothbrushes, leaves for medicine. And its flowers go into a rasam that I don't like because it is bitter. In a corner is a guava tree, with small hard fruit that we covet, though they have no taste.

The inside of the house smells of cooking all the time, especially during the rains, when all the shutters are closed. It smells not just of cooking, but also of smoke from the cooking fire, of the people in the house, often of sweaty clothing, and, on windy days, of the palm-frond thatch above. In summer there is the smell of cowdung from the cowdung-in-water solution that the women apply to the earth inside the house: it smells until it is completely dry. It is a comforting smell, for it reminds you that you are never alone.

We wait for my father to return at dusk. Father works in the fields sometimes to earn a living. His work as a hangman brings little money. When he returns in the evening, soon after sunset, he has his wages with him, a coin or two in his pocket. He gives the money to Mother, who gives me one of the coins and tells me to run up to Ranga's shop to buy tiny quantities of kerosene oil and some chilli powder and salt to use in the night's dinner. Ranga gives me the salt and chilli wrapped in broad teak leaves. Ranga wraps up all little things in those leaves. There is no paper. When we buy jaggery in wet weather, it leaves sweet traces on the leaf, and we lick it though Mother tells us again and again that the rough leaf will cut our tongues.

If there is fish, or meat, which is very rare, then I buy an onion or two as well. If Father doesn't get work, we spend the evening in the dark, for there is no kerosene, and we get only gruel, with salt if we're lucky. Sometimes the grown-ups do without even that. But this evening Father has eight annas, which is quite enough. I see him put away some of that. I wonder why they don't spend all of it on a feast for everyone.

Every year, for Onam, Vishu and for Pongal, we have a feast. Otherwise we have feasts only when someone dies, marries, or bears a child. And what feasts! As much rice as you can eat, and vegetables, and if someone has killed a goat, some mutton as well. We really look forward to the feasts, even those after deaths.

The dark creeps up on me while I'm on my way to Ranga's shop, which is by the roadside, a good kilometre away through the fields. I know these fields well, and tonight the moon is up early, so I go happily, but on darker nights, or rainy nights, I cannot see where I am going. I wish we had a lantern for me to carry when I go to the shop in the dark. I wish to return to the warmth and the comfort of home, where there's Mother to look after us if the terrible yakshis come to get us. She is there to drive the snakes away, the nocturnal vipers and cobras that can kill. She is there to protect us in the dark.

Most nights, Father hasn't the time to make these purchases himself. He has to bathe in the temple pond, pray a little, and chat for a while with his friends who have gathered under the tree outside the temple before returning home. Father is a busy man. People keep their distance from Father. I think they're a little scared of him.

If everyone is scared of Father, why are we so poor? Only the poorest buy their oil and spices daily. Everyone else buys larger quantities. It's cheaper that way. I remember Father explaining that to me, that when you buy a whole sack of rice containing a hundred pounds it's cheaper than buying a hundred pounds of rice one pound at a time.

At the shop Ranga takes my money before giving me what Mother asked me to get. Why? If he is afraid of Father why does he take my money first?

I finished this much that evening, before the light faded. I wanted to read it in the morning before the writer arrived, but he came early. He took the notebook and squinted into it. 'I can't read this,' he said.

I grabbed it from him. 'I'll read it out to you.' I did, and I could see that he understood. 'Now do you see what my childhood was like? Every evening?'

'Yes.' He looked at me strangely.

'So if you see a small half-naked boy asking for a little kerosene at a shop at dusk, let him go quickly. He's hurrying home because he's scared, and because there are people waiting for him. And think of me.'

'I will,' he said. 'I surely will.'

'It's strange,' I said, 'it was only when you asked me about my childhood and I wrote this bit that I remembered how we lived and I understood … I don't think I had really understood till now how poor we were when I was young …'

'That's good, then, keep writing.' He stood up from the lump of concrete. 'I am here for a week and will come again every day. May I do that?'

'Yes, but where are you going?'

'Back to the hotel. To leave you alone to write.'

I remembered something from our first meeting. 'You'd said that you have relatives, on West Car Street.'

'I had an uncle living there,' he replied.

'Has he moved?'

'Yes,' he said heavily. 'To another world.'

'I'm … I'm sorry,' I said. 'You never told me.'

He smiled a crooked smile. 'I didn't want to take your mind off your book.'

'Were you close?'

'Yes.'

'How did he die?'

'Heart attack. I left him one morning to visit Trivandrum. I finished my work there and was at tea at another relative's house when my mother called to say he was gone.'

I sensed some pain in his voice. Why hadn't he told me? 'You should have told me. We are friends now, aren't we?'

'Yes,' he replied. 'I didn't want to bother you, that's all.'

'Next time something of the kind happens, tell me.'

'I will.' He smiled again, faintly, and left. I was beginning to like him.

7

After the writer left I sat with a lump in my throat for a while, for thinking of the little boy had brought many other things to mind.

An old man forgets, but I found that having to write brought back memories I would have thought were long gone. I remembered when Father returned from Trivandrum one evening. He had been gone three days this time and I wanted to tell him about the reminder from school, that my fees were overdue.

He was always grim-faced when he got back from Trivandrum, that much I knew. He was always distant, but there were times when he would play with my brothers and me, swinging us up in the air, sometimes two at a time. These times were fairly regular, even though not common. He was visibly happier on Sundays and holidays, when there was little work to be done—he had a half-day and a little money to spend on it.

That evening when he returned from Trivandrum he was grimmer than usual, and he came alone, without his companions. I didn't know, then, what he did for a living, how we all survived. When I saw him come home, I played tricks, the kind of tricks that any young lad might play to get a father's attention, and this time I found he did not respond. I changed tack, gave up tricks and tried the direct approach.

That didn't work either. Again he didn't respond. It was as if I had slipped out of his world, become invisible. Finally, when I asked if he had brought me anything, he reacted: he told me very brusquely that he had better things to do in Trivandrum than pander to his son's whims. He smelt strange, too; he had been drinking. He rarely sat silent for long, but that evening I remember he spoke not a word to anyone, to Mother or to any of the other children. Mother seemed to understand and didn't worry too much, but I did. I felt left out of his life.

I wondered for a long moment whether it was something particularly bad that I had done that made him so silent. How had I let him down? My father was my hero, I copied every little gesture of his—his slow and measured gait, the way he squinted when looking into the distance. He was my best friend too, and I had no secrets from him. Now, in that one moment in the darkness, I knew that our relationship had changed. There was a distance between us that I would never be able to close. It hurt immensely.

Next morning Father was still asleep when I woke up, and that was strange. He was sleeping on his back, his strong arms lax, and snoring through his open mouth. I remember his breath blowing his moustache up and down, and how that made me laugh.

Much later I found out that he had returned from a hanging, one that hadn't gone well. And then my first thought was this: I hope I never get to be the hangman, for I don't want to do to any of my children what Father happened to do to me that evening. But I didn't worry about it much then, because I was the second brother. My elder brother would take on the job and I would be free to do something else.

~

I am not the first-born son, but I get my father's job.

Not from merit, let me assure you, but because my elder brother Raman has found himself unwilling to hang people for a living. He finds the idea repugnant, and now that the time has come for Father to retire, he says that he will not have Father's job, he would prefer working in the fields and helping out the gurukkal at our temple. There are no secrets in our small houses—Father's and mine—which are next to each other; though they go out into the yard to talk when they discuss it, I can hear them clearly. It's a pleasant February night, cloudless and cool, with the hum of insects and chirp of crickets in the air. This is my favourite time of the year, and I am out in my yard, too, for a smoke.

'So be it,' I hear Father tell Raman. 'If you can't do it, someone else will have to. I will ask Janardhanan to do it.'

'Yes,' Raman replies. 'He might do it. But he is married, and you know how wives are.'

'Wives can be persuaded. It's not as if he's doing something very great now.'

'At least he eats regularly and has a house to live in.'

'We all have that.'

We do, just barely. We merely get by. I am at this time a levy, working occasionally, helping the clerks assess the tax that farmers have to pay. Since tax is mostly on agricultural produce, it is important that we know how much is produced. When the time comes for assessment, I go with the bailiff to measure the grain. It isn't a great job, nor is it secure. Besides, it is not only the king but also the British that I am serving, and in the early 1940s this has its own shame. Already there is talk of Independence, and we know it will come soon. We have a vague idea that the white man will be thrown out and we will live freely. (In those days freedom mattered.) But the real reason I don't like the job is that it makes me hated. Everyone in Parvathipuram knows that I am the hangman's son, and the hangman has some respect, some of which rubs off on me. And since I am a government worker, there is some added respect. But nobody hates my father. They hate me. They hate me because I never falsify records, never take little gifts for telling half-truths.

They might fear the hangman but they don't hate him. The hangman has honour in the village, but not the man who in bad years uses his knowledge of the village to figure out where his neighbours might hide their grain. That, to these people, is the darkest face of the king.

I would rather be a hangman, I think. If Father asks me I will accept. But then, as Raman has rightly said, there is Chellammal to handle. If Father asks me, I will tell him first that I will speak to her. If she accepts the change, there is no problem. Otherwise I will ask Father to speak to her. She will not disobey him, no matter how much she disagrees with him.

Father and Raman finish their little conversation and go to sleep, while I lie tossing and sleepless. If he asks me, I will do the job ...

How will I tell Chellammal?

She is my wife. She has to accept it, any wife must. So far she has not complained about leaving her people and living with me, about the different customs that we follow, about the different food, about having to look after my mother. She has taken it all well, and I think she will understand.

Chellammal called me for lunch, jerking me back to the present. I was disoriented for a moment: when I saw her face I had been thinking of her as she had been more than fifty years ago and I wondered how she had become so old so soon.

Lunch, too, was a surprise. There was chicken, besides the usual rice and sambar. It was for the grandchildren. A small feast, like the ones of my childhood. But there was a further surprise: Chellammal had kept a leg for me. Even after a half-century of marriage she can surprise me.

She did once long ago, when I became the aratchar.

Father calls me out into the yard for a chat early the next morning. He calls me out and very hesitantly says that Raman wouldn't like to be the hangman. I wait quietly for him to continue, and after an uncomfortable pause he goes on. 'We must keep this job in the family,' he says.

'Why?' I ask.

'Because work like this keeps you going during the bad times,' he replies.

'I don't understand,' I say.

'When the rains fail and there is no harvest to be measured, where will you go?'

It would be difficult to manage, I know. 'There will be other work.'

'Not always. You say that now because you have no children, and you are young. I have seen people get into debt in bad years and carry that debt through many generations. This job will help you avoid that. You will eat even during the bad years.'

'Yes,' I agree, for I remember the time when I was growing up—the hangman's family never starved. Even in the worst of times we managed at least one meal a day.

'Your family will never starve, Janardhanan,' Father says.

That was how it used to be in the old days. That was why Father took on the hangman's job in the first place. When the original aratchar family went looking for a poor relative to do their dirty work for them, and found my father, he agreed, because he knew all about hunger. They gave Father a patch of land on which he could build a house, and they gave him three sacks of grain from every harvest, twice a year, telling him that this was his share of the king's grant. They held on to all the land and the wealth. Perhaps Father felt used and cheated. I never knew. He also got his allowances from the prison superintendent when he performed his executions. All told it wasn't very much but it was better than nothing, and it kept the family going in times when many others gave up.

In the bad years we lived on one meal a day. The men in the village were idle, and when they gathered in the evenings to talk, they sounded defeated. In fact, there was a sense of defeat everywhere and at all times. I sensed it first when I was eight, when the summer grew vicious.

That year the mango crop was good, but in those days mangoes weren't for sale. They grew wild, you could walk into anybody's yard and eat your fill of them if you could brave the red ants that swarmed the trees. Early that summer the children gorged on mangoes, basketsful of them.

But then the rains just didn't come. They were due in early June but even in the middle of June the sky was blue and the sun scorched the last bit of moisture out of the topsoil. Even the tall trees that usually stayed green went brown in patches, and the short walk to get drinking water became a daily four-mile hike. The level of water in the temple pond dropped ominously, there wasn't enough even for a proper dip.

On warm evenings the men sat in the dry breeze in the golden light of the setting sun, looking at the earth caked in the fields. I remember—one of them tried to scratch something in the hard soil with a twig, but couldn't make a mark, and the twig broke, and he wept. There was no work anywhere: normally, there would be work for anyone willing, but this year there was none. The moneylender grew wealthy. People pawned their land and ornaments and he loaned them money at extravagant interest, which everyone knew the borrower wouldn't be able to pay. The shopkeeper also grew rich, for the prices of everything went up.

But there was food in the hangman's house. We had rice from the sacks from the last harvest, and there was a little water in the well, enough for cooking. Ranga gave us salt on credit, and we managed in the dark, without kerosene, eating early and going to bed at sunset.

When the rains did come that year it was too late for some who had pawned their jewels or patches of land. The moneylender now had people working on his land, people who were former smallholders. Many children dropped out of school. Families migrated from the village because they had nothing left: some went to Madras, where they had relatives, where they hoped to find work, and others … they just disappeared.

I wondered how those who had left for Madras got there without money for the rail fare. They must have gathered their belongings and walked ... Did they survive? I never heard of them afterwards.

'What will you tell your wife?' Father asks when I agree that being a hangman would keep us secure.

'Just what you told me.'

'She might not like being a hangman's wife.'

'I will persuade her. If she agrees, well and good. If not, well, she'll just have to learn to be a hangman's wife.'

Under normal circumstances, Father would have told her directly, and she would have had to accept it. But she is a Christian, and Father still hasn't got used to it. So he treats her differently from his other daughter-in-law: difficult matters he tells me and I tell her. Not that there have been many such matters in the years since we got married. Getting Father to agree to the marriage was one thing, for he could be stubborn, but once he had agreed, he supported us as best he could, though Chellammal brought no dowry.

In the evening, when there is a lull in her work, I draw Chellammal aside. There is no privacy, so we whisper. 'Listen,' I tell her, 'Father told me something that you should know.'

'What?' she asks. She has this habit of looking at me full in the eye that sometimes makes me uncomfortable. This is a bright night and a large yellow moon smiles down from a cloudless sky. Though I can't see her face clearly, I see her eyes glinting.

'Raman … Raman wants to go on a pilgrimage.'

'What sort of a pilgrimage?' she asks.

'To Kashi.'

'But that'll take a long time, won't it?'

'The way he plans to do it, it could take a few years.'

'So what will his wife do while he is away?'

'Go to her parents.'

'Won't they mind?'

'No, they won't … I don't think so.'

'Why are you telling me all this now?'

'Father is growing old. He wants to give up his work.'

'What work … ?' she begins, her words fading when it sinks in. 'You mean … you mean you'll be the hangman.'

'Yes.'

'Are you telling me this or are you asking if I like it?'

'Both.'

'You mean I'd better like it.'

'Yes.'

'I'll think about it and tell you tomorrow. In the morning.' She returns to her work, helping Mother.

As I wait for her to tell me next morning, I realize how busy she is at that time of the day. She has to help Mother with the housework—for only Father's house has a kitchen—the most important chores being fetching water for the kitchen and getting wood for the fire. By the time she is free it is well past eleven, with a lunch of rice and beans cooking slowly on the fire. She takes a break and comes out into the yard where I sit alone. 'What have you decided?' I ask.

'What is there to decide if you have already chosen?' she snaps. But her anger is playful, I can see, and she is mocking me.

'You must decide whether you like it or not.'

'I have decided not to like it,' she announces. 'But I have no choice.' She turns on her heel and flounces away, then stops for just long enough to turn her head and throw a remark over her shoulder. 'I still remember that your people ate even when everyone else didn't.' And that is that. She says no more about it.

~

Shortly after taking Father's job, in 1941 or so, I went for my first hanging as aratchar.

I don't remember how old I was at the time. In those days we had no birth certificates. Most of us remembered our age by events related to us by our elders: so and so was born the year after the cow calved at midnight, waking everyone up, so and so was born the year Parameswaran's hut burnt down, and so on. So I don't remember exactly how old I was when I went for my first hanging, but I do remember it was in 1941.

After the hanging comes the dark.

It is my first hanging. All through the bus ride home I am tired, and at home I only have the strength to find my way to the bed and lie down. I do not want to talk, for talk hurts. I do not want to listen to talk, because it is an intrusion. For the moment, all I want is silence.

Chellammal does not understand. She keeps asking me if I am well, and offering me coffee or something to eat. She feels my forehead to see if I have a fever, which I don't. Time passes, but not the dark. She calls me for dinner, and I tell her I want none. She insists, and I ignore her, because now I am too tired even to shout at her.

Then I realize that I am not tired. There is a weight sitting in my chest that takes my breath away and leaves me weak. I continue to lie there, listening to the sounds of the others in the other house eating their dinner before preparing for bed.

More time passes, and I hear her footsteps approach. The small lamp goes out and there is only the dim moonlight shining in through the window. Her clothes rustle, and she is beside me, on the mattress, her shoulder to mine. 'What happened?' she whispers.

'Nothing,' I whisper back. It is easier to whisper with a weight on your chest.

I feel her hand upon my chest, and her face upon my shoulder. She moves closer, seeking with her hands and her body the joy that brings us together. But my mind is still on the dark, and I do not respond. I cannot respond. I cannot also find the strength to tell her not to intrude. After a while she moves away, but I can still feel her arm on mine. There is a small comfort there, I do not know why.

Her breath eases and lengthens out. She is tired, and despite everything, sleep comes easily to her. I listen to the sound of her breathing and to the crickets outside and lie wishing for sleep.

Sleep comes, at last, I do not know when. When it passes, it is still dark, but it seems that morning is not far. She has not moved in the night, for I can still feel her arm by mine. There comes the memory of her hands before she went to sleep, and in the dark my body responds. I grip her hand, knowing that her sleep is not deep, for she is not snoring.

She comes awake quickly, whispering, 'What?'

I take her hand and move it down, and turn upon my side, facing her. She is fully awake now, for her eyes glint in the faint light of the stars. Her breathing quickens, and her leg comes up. In the quiet of the morning, there is desire, and a brief burst of joy. When it is over, she does not move away as usual. I feel her hair upon my shoulder, and though I do not speak she knows that the weight on my chest is lighter now.

From somewhere comes the wail of a child. Life must continue. There will be the weight again, perhaps, but it is lighter now. It is bearable. Now I know how Father felt when he returned, and I understand his silence.

~

The following year sticks in my mind. It was 1942, one of our worst years ever. Not that the rains failed: the rains came more or less on time, and in the right quantities, and there was work all round, as usual. But that year the normal daily labourer's wages just weren't enough. Until then, the usual payment of seven chakrams, a quarter of a rupee, for a day's work was enough to feed a family. But that year there was trouble in faraway Burma, and we got no rice from there. Prices rose, and though it was a good year with a reasonable harvest people went without food.

It was a difficult time. Even some of the better-off people stopped sending their children to school. By the end of that year I don't think there was a single girl in the school nearby: when families couldn't afford to send children to school, they always pulled the girls out first. Girls would be married off anyway, people used to think, they didn't need too much learning. It's much the same now in these small places.

The shops had rice only for the well off, and the landless starved. We had rice from the previous year's gift from the king, and we got some credit from the shop. We made it through the year without much trouble, though we did have to subsist on just plain gruel for a few months. It was then that I picked up this taste for rice gruel. Eat it slowly, make it last as long as you can, and it gradually gets sweet in your mouth. Once you learn to like it the taste never leaves you, even though it is the taste of something just short of starvation.

8

All this, about things that happened over half a century ago, I wrote in a week during which the sun grew steadily hotter. In the afternoons it was vicious, burning through the thinning foliage of the tree in the backyard. The wind blew dark, thick clouds of dust into the air, and the hedges browned and wilted. There were more snakes now in the embankments between fields, and the mouths of burrows in the earth, where rats and snakes lived, were clearly visible because the cover of vegetation was gone.

Water comes to the village from the pump, a public borewell, and the queues before it lengthened with the days.

And with the heat came the blackness, for the words stopped.

I still didn't know what it was, that blackness. It was a sort of urge to do something, to finish something, and

I hadn't the faintest idea what I wanted to do. I went walking in the mornings, wrote in the afternoons, and walked again in the evenings. I drank a lot of water, lost my appetite and lost some weight.

I grew irritable. I raised my voice at Chellammal at least thrice that week, and she grumbled at me.

When the writer came again, I told him about the anger. 'I don't know what it's about,' he said. 'You have to find out for yourself.'

'I've been sitting in front of the notebook for the past three days,' I said. 'Now and then I write a word or two, then cut it out ... And I keep losing my temper. What should I do?'

'Nothing. Take a day or two off, then get back to writing. Perhaps it's writer's block. It might clear up as soon as we get back, or it might take years.'

This man is useless, I thought, he's not saying anything useful. I tried to rein in my impatience. 'I hope you can wait all those years for the book,' I snapped, the disgust evident in my voice.

'Leave it,' he said. 'I've told you this before and I say it again. I'll write it, you just answer questions as best you can ...'

'Nonsense,' I snapped. 'This is something I have to do ... How much money do you have with you?'

'A few hundred rupees,' he said, taken aback at this change of tack.

'Give me a hundred, then.'

'Of course.' He kept his money in a leather pouch tied around his waist. He searched through the mess of papers in the pouch until he found a hundred-rupee-note and handed it over. 'Is that enough?'

'Yes, it is,' I replied shortly. I had no idea how he would react if I told him what I wanted it for. I folded the note and tied it up in a corner of my lungi.

He gave me a curious sidelong look. There was something he wanted to ask but wouldn't, and I was glad he wouldn't.

He rose from the lump of concrete that had become his permanent seat when he came visiting. 'Shall I come tomorrow?' he asked.

'All right,' I said, 'but don't expect me to have written anything by then.'

'Fine,' he said. 'I'll be here tomorrow evening, about five.'

All afternoon the note was heavy in my lungi but I do not like to drink in the daytime so I had my lunch quietly and dragged the table out into the hot backyard to keep up the pretence. I was impatient for the evening and the cooling breezes so that I could go to Mahalingam's shop to sit and drink and eat ripe sweet bananas that they say add to the kick of the liquor. The blackness receded, for the liquor was on my mind.

When the sun turned orange and began to sink into the purple hills to the west, I started off. 'Where are you going?' Chellammal asked.

'None of your business,' I snarled at her.

She guessed, of course; after so many years together there are few secrets between us. 'Did you take money from that madman, the writer?' she asked, her voice rising with irritation.

'None of your business,' I snarled again.

'If someone has to carry you back here drunk you can lie outside all night,' she said, and then I was out of earshot. She doesn't like me going out alone these days, and she doesn't like me drinking.

Mahalingam was in his shop, behind the counter with the bottles and plastic pouches of clear fluid. The light was fading but Mahalingam doesn't like too much light: his most profitable business is conducted in the dark. But there was enough light left for me to see his face. 'It's been a long time,' he said when he saw me, smiling warily. 'What can I give you?'

I picked up a pouch. 'A few of these.'

His eyes stayed wary but his smile disappeared. 'When will you pay?'

I took the note from my lungi and tossed it on the counter in front of him. 'In advance if you like.'

The smile returned. 'Sit,' he said. 'Help yourself.'

'Light a lamp,' I told him. 'I have to see what I drink.'

'Of course,' he said. He followed me to the bench where I sat, and on the narrow table in front he put a smoky lamp. He yelled at his helpers—there were two of them—to fetch me some boiled eggs and two glasses. He slit the bag neatly and poured its contents into the glasses, filling them almost to the brim.

I drink very rarely, unlike in my youth, and I have never liked the taste of this raw clear arrack. The only way to drink it is to hold your breath and empty the glass in one quick gulp. I did that and a coughing fit seized me, but the liquor stayed down. I ate a quarter of a boiled egg, loaded with salt and pepper, and then another, and in a few minutes I was ready for the next glass. By this time the blackness was gone as if it had never been, and I was happy and smiling again. The third glass, half an hour later, went down with very little trouble and after that I don't really remember what happened.

Next morning I came awake at my gate, my head spinning and aching, and the nausea strong in my throat. I made it to the backyard, so that people wouldn't see me, and threw up. There I sat wretchedly, unable even to ask Chellammal for a glass of black coffee, or to enter the house. By seven the sun was already warm and when I finally went into the house Chellammal began to nag. 'I told you you'd get drunk,' she said, her voice pitched high, as it is when she is unpleasant. 'You know you shouldn't be doing this and yet you take money from the writer and go off to your favourite shop. I bet you don't even know what you had and how much and whether Mahalingam cheated you.'

'Quiet!' I said. 'Don't shout at me now.'

'When should I shout at you, pray?' Her voice rose. I was sure it could be heard outside on the road, and I was ashamed. 'When you behave yourself or when you come back home in the small hours stinking like a pig?'

I ignored her and found a change of clothes. There was water in the public tap so I took the soapbox and had a long bath, soaping myself thoroughly, and washing my beard, too. I felt much better after that. Murugan had opened his shop so I had some good strong coffee from his first brew of the day. When I went back home I thought Chellammal was waiting to shout at me but she wasn't. She had some rope in her hands, thin white rope that she wanted me to use to repair the broken washing line, which was beyond her reach. I saw the rope and it hit me, a great hammer blow of thought, and I didn't hear her words when she spoke them, even though I was looking at her and could see her mouth working.

She had to repeat herself twice before I understood. I did what she wanted me to, and then found my writing table and dragged it out into the backyard. I settled down to write and found the words coming. They came slowly, but they came, and I was relieved.

The rope is part of the ritual. It is white and soft, and its fibres come apart easily. But then it's meant to be used only a very few times.

The law says that at least three ropes have to be available at every hanging. Each rope has to be tested the day before the hanging, with a weight at least one-and-a-half times the condemned man's weight. I am responsible for all that testing. A rope might be tested three or four times at most, before it is used to hang a man. Five times, then, at the most: it won't be used again after that.

In the old days there used to be even more ritual. The hangman prepared the rope himself. It had to take the knot easily, the slip knot that tightened about the condemned man's neck. In my father's day the hangman used butter to grease the rope, and to soften it so it would knot easily. First he wet the end of the rope that went about the neck, then dried it and used up to a pound of butter to grease it, making sure that the butter got properly into the fibre. There are stories that the rope was also dipped in milk, and so on, but as best I know they used only butter or clarified butter, and the purpose was only to make the rope soft and pliable. Butter attracts rats, so the ropes used to be kept in airtight wooden boxes and were taken out only minutes before they were tested. Then they went back into the boxes, to stay there until minutes before the hanging, when the hangman selected a rope.

Ropes used to be made of a special fibre from the fronds of a palm—I don't know which one. Afterwards they began ordering rope from a factory far away, somewhere in Bengal, from a company called Shalimar, I think. And now convicts make the ropes while they serve out their sentences. So it is possible that someday a man will be hanged to death by a rope he himself has made.

The rope today, spun and woven by convicts in the prison workshop, is just soft cotton rope. It slips easily around the condemned man's neck, and when I tighten the knot so the noose fits snugly about the man's neck, I know it will stay in place and do the job it should.

After the man is dead the rope is mine. It is supposed to be mine, at any rate, but I get only a small part of it. Others compete for pieces of the hangman's rope—the prison staff and often the visitors, or the visitors' underlings. The rope, they say, is valuable, as long as it has been used to kill a man.

They say many things about the rope. Keep a small bit in your house and it will protect you from disaster. Tie a strand of it on a baby's cradle and the baby will have no nightmares; it will be safe from evil spirits, from the bhoothams and prethams that come alive after dark. I remember Father telling me long ago that he used to tie a bit of his rope to our cradles.

So the jail staff collect bits of rope to take home, and perhaps to sell. Over the years I have heard of more things for which the rope is used. One story says, burn a small length of a strand of the rope. Dissolve the remnants in honey. Given to children to drink, this concoction cures stomach disorders.

But perhaps the strangest of them all is something that Maash told me, something from a book that he called the *Raja Marthandam.* I remember the name of the book because it is so similar to that of king Marthanda Varma, the king who appointed one of my ancestors his hangman. This book offers a cure for epilepsy. Burn a length of the hangman's rope, it says, and collect the soot from the fire. Mix the soot thoroughly in plain water, and you will get a black liquid. Drinking this black liquid will cure an epileptic.

I have thought many times of how these strange

recipes originated. I don't know if they work: I tied bits of rope to the cradles of my own children, but they cried and did all the normal things that babies do. The other things I never tried, because we had our own remedies.

I think these stories about the powers of the hangman's rope were made up by hangmen who felt they had to do something to raise their status in society. If this was their objective, I can tell you that they didn't succeed.

9

When the writer came in the evening I was only a paragraph into the story of the rope. I was still bent over the table and he came around to the back and squatted on the ground facing me across my small table. 'It appears the words are coming again,' he said.

'They are,' I told him.

Chellammal must have seen him coming, for she came around the corner of the house just then. She had a load of dry clothes over one arm, just taken down from the washing line I'd fixed in the morning. 'Why did you give him money?' she asked him. There was an aggressive note in her voice and she had her head thrust forward as she does when she's looking for a fight.

'He asked for it,' the writer said. 'Why? Was it wrong to do that?'

'Of course not,' she flared at him. 'It was a fine thing to do. It was a fine thing to give him money so that he could spend last night drinking with his old buddies. They brought him back at two in the morning. They had to carry him, and he threw up all over the gate. And who do you think has the privilege of cleaning up?'

'I didn't know,' he told her. 'I had no idea what he wanted the money for ... In any case, I owe him some, for what he's doing with the book.'

'He's done nothing!' She paused for a moment to take a deep breath. 'He just sits around here and scribbles all afternoon, and he doesn't eat on time.'

I felt anger rise in me. Chellammal had gone too far with this. I would not permit her to yell at my friends in my own house. 'Shut up, woman,' I told her. 'It's not his fault. If you want to blame someone blame me. And do it after he leaves.'

She glared at me for a moment, then turned on her heel and walked off in a huff. 'I apologize for her behaviour,' I told the writer.

'So did you really have to be carried back in the morning?' he asked.

'Yes,' I admitted. I was still feeling a little sheepish about it. I would have been much more sheepish about it if I hadn't managed to write a little after that. 'But it worked.'

'What worked?'

'The liquor. The words are coming.' I showed him the book, with the lone paragraph. 'This is about the rope. I'll finish it today or tomorrow.'

'I've heard about the rope,' he said.

'I'll give you some. For you to keep. It might bring you luck.'

'Yes,' he smiled. 'I'd like that.' Inside the house I found the plastic carrier bag in which I kept several lengths of rope that had loosened up into something that looked like white cotton waste. The fibres had all come apart and got badly tangled. I took the pile out into the sun and snipped off a bit for him, just a little bit. He stuffed it into the pouch at his waist and thanked me. 'Do you remember whose hanging this rope came from?' he asked.

'It could be from any of several,' I told him. 'I used to take a piece of every rope and put it in this bag. They're all mixed up.'

He looked at his feet for a while. 'All right,' he said. 'The question I really want to ask is this: is there a hanging that you remember better than the rest, for any reason at all?'

'Difficult question,' I told him. 'There are a few, of course, but some of them I remember for other reasons.'

'Other reasons such as what?'

'Such as having to give up my annual pilgrimage one year because there were two hangings during the vratam.'

'What vratam?'

'The one for Sabarimala.' Every year after my third daughter died I used to try to go to Sabarimala, as a sort of diksha, a penance. This meant a six-week regimen of no smoking, no drinking, no meat ... And no hangings, because killing is forbidden. One year when the summons came three weeks into the vratam I wondered what to do because I didn't want to break my vratam, and I didn't want to neglect my duty. Chellammal's brother Ambrose, who is my height, and thin and bearded like me, offered to go in my place, and I considered taking him up on it, but didn't. That year I missed Sabarimala.

'Are you religious?' the writer asked. 'Do you believe in god?'

'When you put it like that ... I suppose I am,' I replied. I've always accepted the existence of god: that was the way we were brought up. There are times, though, when I believe otherwise, that there cannot be a god, that death is just an endless sleep, and there is no rebirth, no release, no hope. 'I've never thought about it very much.'

He left soon, but it was too late then to write. I sat in the dark in the backyard, hardly noticing the mosquitoes that swarmed up from a nearby pond.

That night I had the nightmare again, the one about the gallows and the man with the flat black mask for a face. In the morning the blackness was back, stronger than ever. But the words were there, and through the morning I used the pen to fight the blackness off.

We walk through the night and rest in daylight, in the shade of a tree. The December sun is warm and pleasant, but we are too tired to think. We spread our black lungis on the ground and no matter how rough or hard the surface we are all asleep in minutes.

We are a motley group of six devotees from Nagercoil. We took the bus to Trivandrum, and another bus from there to Quilon. From Quilon we have walked. It is no great hardship when you have the right company. There is some boredom, but when you walk all day, when you bear your small bundle of belongings on your head and try to cover thirty or forty miles a day, very soon only the walk remains. Your life becomes the step, the process of putting your foot on the ground, of pulling your other leg forward for the next step, and the next, and the next, and so on. Each step is the same in the sense that each day is the same. When you are into the pilgrimage, reciting the prayer over and over again, that is all there is.

The past six weeks have been difficult. We have not smoked or had a drink or eaten meat. There are other restrictions on what we eat and we have all lost a little weight. In a sense the vratam is purifying.

But this is the first time I have ever asked myself: why am I here? Why am I on this long walk through forests and up the hill to the mosque and past that to the temple, for a bath in a river, where an old lady was supposed to have been blessed by Rama? Why, when I don't even know if I believe in Rama himself?

I don't know. I have a vague faith that god will take care of me, that life will not be too painful. That is all I really hope for. I have been coming this way every year after my third daughter died in her youth. It is a penance.

A penance? For what? What guilt brings me here? Can I believe the myth that some hangman created long ago about the good that comes from the hangman's rope?

These things have been troubling me for some time now. Death will come to all of us, as it came to my daughter, before her time. What difference does this annual pilgrimage make? Will it save anyone? Will it delay anyone's death? Will it save anyone an instant's pain? Or am I just driven to do this? Am I a wisp of smoke to be blown about by the winds of fate?

I wish I knew. This question will come up again, I know, for it is there in every moment of my life, and I only evade it.

What am I doing?

I knew the blackness no better after I started putting down my memories, but at least I knew that it was nothing recent. It started long ago on one of those pilgrimages … No, perhaps it started earlier.

I wished I remembered when exactly the blackness first made itself felt. Sometimes I felt as if it were new every moment and at others as if it had been with me all my life. Most of the time I felt that my life had been spent running away from it, and that it was finally catching up.

The only refuge in recent months came from liquor: when I went and got thoroughly drunk it did not bother me. Or I had no memory of being bothered by it, which was perhaps different, but at least it enabled me to sleep.

10

'Tell me about your family,' the writer asked. 'What do your brothers do now?'

'Raman is gone ... His children don't write, we don't have the habit. But we meet once in a while, at festivals or weddings or funerals. Paraman lives nearby. He never married, and he lives alone. He's the caretaker of a small house here.'

'In those days large families were common ... It's strange that you had only two brothers.'

'Yes,' I said. 'Mother was ill sometimes, I suppose that must be why. I never thought of it.'

'Write about it, then. I'd like to know.'

He told me a bit about how to recall an image, to concentrate on it and write it out. Then he finished his coffee, and as he got up to leave, something popped into my mind. A small memory of someone challenging my father. A friend of his who said, 'Guess my weight. If you get it right, to within a kilogram, I'll admit you're a better judge of weight than I am.'

Father won his bet that day. That was, after all, part of his job, guessing a man's weight. I, too, learnt it. 'Guess what,' I told the writer. 'I just remembered something.'

He stopped, then sat back down on the concrete. 'What?' he asked.

'You weigh eighty-six kilos.'

'A little more, actually,' the writer replied. 'But you're only a kilo away.'

'Right. And you're ... Ummm ...' I stopped. I can no longer calculate as fast as I used to. 'Shall I say how tall you are, in feet and inches?'

'Of course,' he smiled.

'Five feet nine inches. A little more, maybe, but less than five ten.'

His jaw dropped. 'That's pretty exact,' he said. 'How did you get that close?'

'Practice,' I replied. I had done it over a hundred times, after all. These judgments were the heart of the hangman's art.

The drop. The drop was everything. I wrote about it. I wrote what I could about it, and was happy with what I wrote. So I copied it out separately, and when the writer came next I gave him the clean copy I had made. 'This is for you to keep,' I told him. 'This is the best of what I've done so far.' He read it carefully, not struggling too much with the Tamil script, I could see.

He finished it and said nothing. He folded the sheet and put it in his shirt pocket. He kept that piece. I knew it was good.

~

After I wrote about the drop I found that I could not think of anything to write.

I told the writer about this. He came regularly, and we went for longer and longer walks as the days grew longer. There was no sign yet of the rains: memories came, of long scorching summers, but they were only memories. Few starved these days. On these walks we kept quiet most of the time, talking rarely of writing, but mostly of other matters that he thought might help me find something in my mind worth writing about.

'Next time I come,' the writer said one day, 'will you show me where you met your teacher? Show me your favourite places. Would you like that?'

'Yes. We'll do that. I might remember things … But why wait for next time? Let's go now, for a bus ride.'

'Where?' he asked, a little surprised by my enthusiasm.

'To a temple. To meet a friend.'

'Which temple?'

'A Bhadrakali temple. The one where we used to go before a hanging. We'll meet the ringmaster in one of the little sideshows.'

We walked back along the canal to Parvathipuram. The packed earth road beside the canal joined the main road near a bridge, which is only a couple of hundred yards from the bus stand. At the bus stand we found the bus we would take, Number 31, which takes a circular route, starting here, going on to the bus stand at Vadassery, and returning here for a fifteen-minute break before starting off again. At this point the bus is usually empty; further on it fills up.

The bus started with a jerk, and all the seats filled up at the first stop, near the bridge. It proceeded jerkily on, getting more and more crowded, and when the conductor came along to give us tickets he had to push his way through a thick crowd. We shoved our way out of the bus at Vadassery, and from the junction near the bus stand we took the road that curves downwards towards SMRV school, one of the oldest schools in the district. About a quarter-mile down the road we took a lane to the right, a narrow, crooked, cramped lane, down which we could see rows of cramped old houses. All the buildings in this area seemed ancient—whitewashed squat buildings with tiled roofs blackened by the sun and the rain, and tiny windows fitted with wooden bars.

When I passed through here I went back twenty years in time, it had changed so little. We went past the school, which was built in the nineteenth century, and the bunch of old houses, then round a corner where there were fields to the west and a tiny temple to the right.

The temple door was shut, and a man in a small shop—a new one, less than five years old—at the corner told us to come back next morning. But this was familiar territory for me. I had been visiting this place off and on for the past nearly seventy years, and the older people knew me. We went around to the side of the temple compound, and I opened the small rusty gate at the side.

The gurukkal wasn't there but his wife was. This wasn't my gurukkal, of course—Ramayyan Gurukkal, who had been the priest here during my father's day. Ramayyan was gone now. When I replaced my father as the aratchar, he was the one I could visit any time. Ramayyan's son Kuppan runs the show these days, but he doesn't have the depth or the devotion of his father. I introduced the two, the writer and Kuppan, and the writer asked the gurukkal to do a small puja in his name. I saw a fifty-rupee-note change hands, and Kuppan bent to put it away. In the moment he bent over he looked exactly like his father.

I miss Ramayyan. He was one of those, like Maash, who made the silence bearable. I still remember the first time I saw him. I was a child then.

The temple is dedicated to our deity, Bhadrakali, the angry face of Parvati, wife of Shiva. This is my first visit to the temple. I am with my father, and he is going there to sacrifice a rooster to the goddess before going to a hanging, as is the hangman's custom of the day.

I don't understand why he is taking us along, me and my elder brother Raman. But we go without protest, because he takes us out so rarely that any outing with him is a pleasure. We are usually in bed by nine in the evening and up by six, but on this chill morning Father has woken us at four, when the starlight is still bright and the moon long gone. He has woken Mother, too, and she has coffee ready, coffee to wake us up, coffee so hot that it scalds my mouth.

We bathe in the pond, finding our way by the bright starlight. As we wash we disturb the moorhens that nest at the far end of the pond, and they in turn wake the crows roosting in a tree nearby. I start when the cacophony shatters the stillness of the morning, and drop the slippery soap in the dark, cool water. Father puts his hand in the water and finds the soap, handing it to me without a word.

We finish our bath and leave home before dawn, clothed in fresh clothes, new off-white mundus for both Raman and me. We walk half-blind in the deepening mist of December, through the paddy fields to the broad tarred road which leads to town and to my school. Father carries a large white rooster by its legs—its wings and legs are tied together—and we can hear it cluck in bewilderment.

The road is deserted at this time, but as we walk we see the dim lights of faraway kerosene lamps in huts by the fields: people are coming awake. In the mist the dark is menacing, and I hold on to Father's thick and callused thumb for fear of losing sight of him. From this point, where we reach the tarred road, it is six kilometres to the temple, which lies by the fields near SMRV school, which is older than the prison at Poojapura, Father's workplace.

We reach the temple just after first light, the mist beginning to lighten in the faint sunshine. A slice of golden sun above the fields lights up the moment of excitement: I look forward to sharing something—anything—with my father, for it is a sign of growing up.

The temple door is closed but Ramayyan Gurukkal lives right next to the temple, in a two-room house with a low-roofed verandah in front and basil growing by the gate. Father coughs as he swings the small cane gate open, and Ramayyan comes to the door to see who it is. I hesitate at the gate. Father takes my hand to lead me in. The touch of his hand, hard and square and at that moment incredibly gentle, is reassuring, and I follow him in without fear.

The six adiyaans are already here, some of them are members of the original aratchar line. Father said last night that they had already done a puja at their own temple in Bimaneri, where the family's ceremonial sword is kept. They are aloof, their manner a strange mixture of respect and contempt that I don't understand. They don't seem to respect Father much and that I can't understand at all. I wonder why Father tolerates them. In his place, I would not speak to them. I wouldn't even let them into the temple to watch.

The flames in the brass lamps in the shrine flicker in the breeze as Father smears ash on his forehead before bowing to the fearsome icon of the goddess. Ramayyan Gurukkal, young and recently married, speaks to him briefly. He goes into his house and brings out a little cloth-wrapped bundle of flowers, and Father hands him a bottle of liquor and the rooster.

Ramayyan is short and stocky, with his stiff hair cropped short. He has sandal and ash on his chest and upper arms and on his forehead. He wears a thin cloth towel wrapped firmly about his waist, it is so thin that one can make out the outline of the loincloth that he wears under it. His chest is bare and hairless, and he has a few days' stubble on his face. He holds the bottle and the rooster before him in his square, strong hands and mutters some mantras in Sanskrit. When he stoops to put the bottle down he bends smoothly at the waist. Over the rooster he says some more words in Sanskrit before handing it back to Father.

I have seen a rooster being killed before—on feast days, a cousin or even my father would wring its neck in the backyard. One moment the creature would be alive, and dead the next. But what I see at the Bhadrakali temple is strange. Father holds the rooster between his legs, with its feet under his own and its head in his left hand. Then, suddenly, he beheads the rooster cleanly with a single diagonal stroke of a large knife that the gurukkal has given him. The head comes away in his hand.

I have always thought that a rooster would lie still after having its head cut off. But it doesn't: in the dim light the blood spurts blackly from its neck, and its wings flap, strongly at first, then weakly as its lifeblood ebbs away. I step back in fear: here is a dead creature showing all the signs of life.

Father still has the rooster's feet firmly under his own. If he were to let go, I'm sure the headless rooster will run blindly away. Even with him holding on, it struggles for several minutes while the gurukkal chants his violent mantras, the like of which I have not heard at any other temple. His breath comes in brief explosions as he speaks the first syllables of the invocation of Bhadrakali. I can see the strange wildness in his eyes and I shrink from it.

The puja takes an hour. When I have got over my fear, the chanting and the fresh blood on the ground seem inconsequential: the sun is up, and the herons feeding in the fields outside seem more important. After the puja Father rises from his seat on the floor. Ramayyan stands up before him and blesses him, and then the rope that Father had put in his bag, with the bottle, as we left home. By this time it is broad daylight and when we go out, to Ramayyan's house, I can feel the warmth of the sun on my back bringing out sweat. Ramayyan's wife offers my brother Raman a banana for the two of us to share, and we sit on a cot in the long verandah outside the house to eat it.

Father puts the rope back in the little bundle that he carries with him to hangings. The bundle contains what little he will need for a night at the guest house in Trivandrum, including a fresh shirt. He never carries a toothbrush because he prefers a veppu twig instead, or a fistful of charred rice husk which is commonly used in these parts.

He picks up the rooster, too. Later in the day it will

be cooked. Father will have a share of it, and of the contents of the bottle.

Father leads us back home to where Mother waits nervously. 'Give them coffee,' he tells her. 'They watched it quietly. They'll learn.'

After he leaves I think of what he did to the rooster. I have got over my fear, and wish that I could behead a rooster the way Father did it, with a single clean stroke of the knife. I decide that I will do it one day, no matter what I do for a living.

After I became a hangman I performed this ceremony with the rooster a hundred and seventeen times. As a boy I had wanted to behead a rooster as expertly as my father did. But thinking of the times when I went to the temple before the hangings, I remember looking at my adiyaans standing lined up with me, and the people from the original aratchar family, and wishing I didn't have to do it. But it was part of the ritual, and I went through with it for form's sake.

For form's sake? I'm not so sure.

11

Maash lives on in my mind. He was one of the very few people I could call a well-wisher in the best sense of the word.

He died a few years ago, in '87, at the age of eighty. He had a long life and I am sure his working life was fruitful, for most of his students have done very well. He used to take some pride in it, in telling me what his students were doing and how much pleasure they gave him when they visited him.

I don't remember him doing any of his students a favour, though. He was as upright as could be, and I remember him refusing an offer to give a fellow-student of mine a little extra coaching on the side. 'If I teach your son at home,' he said, 'it means that I am not doing justice to the class.'

This despite an offer of ten rupees a month: almost his salary as a teacher. It would have made his life much more comfortable. But he turned it down. I asked him about it later, when I thought I could. It was on one of our walks together, when I was enough at peace with myself to listen and not want only to talk. 'Why did you do that?' I asked him. 'You would have been much better off now if you'd taken the money then.'

'Yes, I would. I could have had a better house,' he said, 'and maybe a little something even to keep my wife quiet. But let me tell you, Janardhanan, if I had taken any of that money my own mind would be making a bigger racket now than my wife ever did.' We walked some more, and he gave me something to think about. 'It's better to follow the rules, generally, because trouble makes you tougher.'

I followed rules too, meticulously, and perhaps that had made me tougher. But who would respect or reward me for being straight and sincere in my job? What temptation can a hangman refuse? What dignity will he earn?

Maash had dignity. His students respected and remembered him. They came to meet him years after having left school. He used to tell me about those visits. He used to tell me, too, about his troubles with his memory. 'Sometimes a student comes and I know he is my student but I can't put a name to him. I feel so ashamed of myself!' he moaned one evening.

'Does it matter?' I asked. 'You had hundreds of students. How can you remember all of them?'

'How can you forget children whose names you have called out in roll call for many years?' he countered.

I don't remember the names of my adiyaans. A few

come to mind. There was Selvan, and Lakshmanan, and ... I forget. But they worked with me for many years, some for decades. I remember their faces, but not their names. Just like Maash.

Where are they? What do they do?

We take the bus together. The adiyaans meet me at the temple, after I have performed the rites that are as much my duty as the execution, and we are ready to go.

There are six of them, as always. An execution is a highly organized matter, and each of us has something very specific to do. The bus at this time of the morning is only half-full and we get seats, though not all together. The bus fills up over the next two or three stops and the silence is shattered by the conversation of commuters. They greet each other like sparrows and the noise intrudes on our silence.

We make no noise, we do not talk, yet the condemned man draws us closer than any other bond does. We are outcasts in a sense, doing society's dirty work for them. I wonder how the others on the bus would react if they knew we are on our way to a hanging.

The adiyaans are mostly family. In the old days it made sense to keep these things in the family, for work was hard to get. Without work, we starved. If we could make sure that someone in the family was going to be fed and taken care of for a few days every now and then, we did it without hesitation. There is a new word for it now: nepotism. Giving work to your relatives.

They make it out to be a bad thing, and it might well be so. But people who make these judgements forget that survival can be difficult. We know that there isn't enough for everyone, and if someone has to starve, it is better that he be outside the clan.

So the adiyaans are mostly family, with a few close friends—almost family. I watch them covertly. Muthu is nineteen, a tall young lad, and very nimble. He passes the rope over the gallows: his height and agility enable him to do things others can't. His cheekbones are prominent and his long hair flutters in the wind. His eyes are gentle, and sometimes I worry about him. He doesn't like to see death. But his parents are gone, he has not gone to school ... Who will give him work? He gets by, helping out in the fields, but when the harvest is over he has nothing to do.

Sometimes I wonder if I am doing the right thing by him. Without this work he would have been forced to do something else. There is no question of his studying, of course, because he can't afford it ... But perhaps he needn't have been stuck with being an adiyaan for the rest of his life, doing something that I can see he detests.

Muthu's grandfather and my father were close friends, and I think there is a small debt that I owe him. This is how our society works. From the time you are born you begin to build up a sort of account of little obligations and favours and gifts, all of which have to be paid back. Sometimes it is a good thing, but now I think it is not. If I had ignored the history and refused to let Muthu work with me he would probably have been better off than he is now. Poor fellow.

So these lists of obligations and favours form a safety net of sorts, one that prevents you from falling to destruction. But its existence also prevents you from seeking your best: I wonder—if I had not been a hangman, what would I have been?

~

I have never travelled much. The only times I have been away for more than ten days at a time is when I went on pilgrimages to Sabarimala. That aside, I have only been away, for a day or two at a time, to attend a wedding or a funeral, or to do a hanging. I have never been out of this province or heard much of any language other than Tamil and Malayalam.

I have never read much, either: it does not come easily. So you might say with some truth that I am an average man from an average small town in South India. But if at all I am any different from the ordinary, the reason is my work, and my contact with people like Maash. He made me think.

After our paths crossed for the second time, Maash and I became good friends. Maash continued to read after his retirement. When he found that I was a hangman, he went to all the libraries nearby to read what he could about executions and executioners all around the world and told me stories about them. His stories were true, because I knew Maash had no need to make up stories to get my attention. He often muttered about the inaccuracy of the writings of a famous traveller named Marco Polo: Polo said that elephants stamped the heads off condemned men in twelfth-century Travancore. 'It's a pack of lies,' Maash would say, with a derisive little snort. 'They used elephants in executions to tear people apart, like they used horses to draw and quarter people in Marco Polo's own country. But using them to stamp down the heads of condemned men? Never!'

Once after telling me this he went silent for a while. 'Janardhanan,' he said pensively later, 'Marco Polo was wrong about the elephants but sometimes I feel we used to be a horrible lot, killing people in horrible ways, and we used to glorify it. Have you heard of a poem called "Sri Krishna Vilasam"? You wouldn't have. You never learnt Sanskrit at school.

'The poem tells the story of a guru and his shishya. The guru used to drive the disciple mercilessly, and treat him far worse than the youngster thought he deserved. A time came when the disciple felt he could bear it no longer, and he decided to do away with his guru.

'He had no poison or weapons, and the guru was surrounded by his disciples all day. So he decided to hide under the eaves of the roof of the guru's bedroom and kill him at night by dropping a large stone on him. After dark one evening he slipped away and made his way to the roof, armed with his large stone, and hid waiting for the man he wanted to kill.

'The guru came after dinner, with his wife. As they prepared for sleep they chatted, as any couple would, and the guru's wife asked her husband, "Why do you treat that disciple of yours so badly?"

'The guru replied placidly, "He is the best of disciples, and he will learn much from his troubles. When he has learnt, I will tell him the truth about himself."

'In the roof above them the shishya shivered. He had nearly killed this man, he thought. What a lucky escape! He clambered down from his hiding place and sneaked into his hut, where he stayed awake through the night thinking of what he should do.

'By morning he knew. He went to his guru and said, "I have a question for you."

'"Ask," said the guru.

'The shishya asked, "If a shishya, feeling that his guru was being unfair with him, decided to do away with his guru, what punishment would be meted out to him?"

'The guru quoted the scriptures, which said that such a shishya should be made to stand in a large pit which would then be filled with paddy husk. The paddy husk would then be set alight, and in its embers the shishya would die a slow and painful death as his body burnt away.

'The shishya then imposed this punishment on himself. He dug a pit, arranged for the right quantity of husk, and had someone light it for him. The guru tried to stop his student from killing himself, but the boy insisted on dying thus. The shishya, they say, composed and recited this poem while being cooked. They say that he stopped reciting at the sixty-fourth stanza because his tongue was burnt away ...'

'Very touching,' I said. 'And very cruel.'

'Cruel, yes,' Maash said, 'but also very short-sighted and unjust. Why should a man be punished for contemplating a crime? Doesn't that make us all criminals? Why didn't the guru say something like this: "All right, you thought of killing me, and now I think of punishing you as prescribed in the scriptures. Now let's get back to this business of dealing with life."'

'Yes,' I said.

'See how cruel we can be? Compared to all that, you're doing a very good job. A painless one.'

'I don't know,' I said. 'A killing is a killing whether painful or not.'

'I think not!' he said firmly.

'Why not?' I asked timidly.

He stopped for several minutes when I said this, and when we resumed our walk it was clear that he hadn't thought it through. We walked in silence for a quarter of an hour and then he spoke. 'That's a very good question ... I'm glad you asked it. Because it's not just one court that decides. A Sessions Court passes the death sentence first. Then the case goes to the High Court of the state. If the High Court upholds the sentence the case goes to the Supreme Court. If the Supreme Court, too, upholds the sentence, they send a mercy petition to the President. In the old days they could send a mercy petition to the state's governor, too, but now that's been stopped. It's only if all these people—not just a single judge—agree that the sentence is fair that you hang anyone.'

'With so many people ... Do you think it's possible they all make a mistake?'

'It's possible, but very unlikely. But let me ask you: have you ever thought that you were hanging an innocent man?'

I thought of it for a while. The mask went over the condemned man's face only when he stood on the trapdoor. I tried always to avoid looking into the eyes of the condemned man, but inevitably I would. The eyes were always inward-looking when I happened to see them. Always, without exception. The men could all be innocent. Or guilty. I never knew which.

Only the condemned man would know what was in his own mind. But at least the judges tried to find out. Yes, I thought in my heart, everyone I have hanged had gone through a certain judicial procedure which established with some certainty that the condemned man had committed the crime for which he was punished, and that the crime he had committed deserved the death penalty.

I used to feel much better listening to Maash talking about these matters. It established a strange bond between the two of us. When he died I think I mourned his passing as much as any of his children.

~

Of Maash's two best stories, one is about the electric chair. This is the fifth time he is relating it to me. I don't mind, because I like to listen to it almost as much as he likes to tell it.

'It was all about business,' he says. 'Two men of the last century who thought that the electric chair would fetch them pots of money—George Westinghouse and Thomas Edison. Everyone who has been to school knows that Edison invented the light bulb, but how many know that he built the first electric chair for money?'

I nod. I have heard this story before, but it still amazes me, what people will do for money.

'Edison and Westinghouse, they competed for the chair. There were no standards for electricity in those days, and Edison was trying to persuade everyone to use DC for gadgets while Westinghouse preferred AC. One of the reasons why Edison preferred DC for gadgets, including the electric chair, was this: AC was more lethal to living beings, and he showed this using stray cats and dogs and one orangutan.

'Edison won that contract on the strength of those demonstrations. The big day came. On 6 August 1890, the first electric chair was readied for use, on a prisoner called William Kemmler.

'Every witness said it was terrible. Kemmler died slowly, and his corpse was cooked as they watched, making many vomit. Others swooned. They all later said that the smell stayed in their noses for days afterwards. And Westinghouse had the last word on that occasion.' Here Maash pauses to get the accent exactly right, and, after a deep breath, continues, '"It would've been better with an axe."'

12

The writer came in a hurry once, in the afternoon, while I was writing. It was May, and again this year, as in most years, there were no signs of early rain. 'I have to go back home for a few weeks,' he explained. 'I'll be back next month.'

'Go,' I said. 'I'll be here.'

'Will you keep writing your journal?'

'Of course I will, now that I've started. But give me your address before you go. Just in case I need to get in touch with you.'

'Of course.'

I brought out the plastic-covered book, a 1966 diary, in which we keep all kinds of family details—addresses, dates of birth, names, everything. It was falling to pieces but the effort of copying its contents into a new book would be defeating, so we continued with the old one. 'I'll write my address in it in English,' he said, 'because if you address a letter to me in Tamil it won't reach me.'

'All right,' I said. 'I can get hold of someone to address it for me if need be.'

'Good.' He paused in some discomfort. 'Would you like some money?'

It was obvious he remembered Chellammal shouting at him and I grinned to reassure him. 'No,' I said. 'The money we will sort out afterwards.'

'All right, then.' He held out his hand.

I had never shaken hands his way. It is not common in our society among people of my generation, and in any case few people would have been willing to shake hands with a hangman. So I took his hand clumsily, and he gripped mine tightly. 'Take care,' he said. 'You're doing fine.'

'Okay,' I replied. 'Will the lady come with you?'

'No,' he said. 'She's no longer necessary, and she has other things to do. A family to look after.'

I was curious but didn't want to pry into his life. He walked off and I watched his feet raising the dust on that May afternoon and suddenly felt bereft. No one else had bothered to look at my life the way he was, and that alone touched me.

But Maash had told me long ago that executioners were not everywhere outcasts from normal society. There were countries that were proud of their hangmen, and there were hangmen who were famous and colourful characters.

There were times when elsewhere executions were performed in public, and people came to watch. I have heard of these public executions being conducted even now. They say that in some mid-eastern countries adultery is still punishable by death, and people are encouraged to stone the erring couple to death. Crowds come to watch, as if they are going to a circus, and sometimes they participate: their government provides them truckloads of stones for the purpose.

Looking back, I know why Maash told me all this so many times, why he repeated the tales of executions in other places, at other times. Compared to the ways in which some of our more outstanding tyrants have got rid of enemies, what I used to do was painless: he was saying that there has always been worse, and there always will be.

As I watched the writer's back disappear around a corner I thought I had much to say about these tales that Maash told me, but when I sat down the next morning to write, the words didn't come easily. I had got used to the writer coming around every now and then to look at what I had done. Knowing he wouldn't be around made writing a burden.

But then I remembered what he had told me, about keeping at the words until something happened. So I wrote, and hoped that he would find it good, though I myself found it confusing, like one of my talks with Maash when he was an old man.

Even in his seventies, Maash is vigorous. He continues his evening walks, though it is now only five kilometres a day. He completes his walk in about an hour, a little slower than before. His once-thick hair is shorn close to the scalp, and he shaves only once a week, leaving a fuzzy stubble about his cheeks most days. He has shrunk some more with the years, and his white shirts hang loosely about him: he has given up the threadbare black jacket, or perhaps it deteriorated so much that he felt he could not wear it any longer. He looks like a scarecrow in his baggy clothes, and vulnerable and poor, as if he has borrowed someone else's clothes. But his back is still straight, and his mind sharp as ever. He stumbles once in a while, and is glad of the support of my arm when he does. In that, too, he has changed: he is less fiercely independent in the presence of those he has known for a long time. And there are long silences, because unlike most other old men he speaks less as he grows older.

'Do you know how the word aratchar came to be?' he asks.

'No,' I reply. 'I never thought about it.'

'I'll tell you,' he says. 'I looked it up in a dictionary. It comes from aratchi, meaning supervision, or investigation. To this was added the ar, the honorific suffix. Aratchar. It should mean honourable supervisor or inspector, but that's not what it has come to mean: now, for all practical purposes, it means hatchet man. The executioner.' We reach a small, low climb, and his breathing becomes a little laboured and his stride shortens. At the top of the climb he takes a deep breath and stops for a second. 'I always wondered what you thought of your work,' he says. 'I never got around to asking you because I thought it was one of those private areas of your mind that you wouldn't like to share.'

'Why do you ask me now?' I ask.

He grins crookedly. His teeth are all gone but he has a fine set of false teeth so his smile flashes more brightly than it did five years ago. 'Now that I am approaching my thousandth month, I feel I've earned the right to ask people rude questions.'

'I don't know what to feel about the job,' I tell him. It's true, and like some truths it surprises me when it emerges. 'Everyone else knows some other person who does the same job, so they can share, and exchange experiences. I can't do that. I can't discuss knots and ropes and trapdoors and masks with anyone else, so I don't really know.'

'I never looked at it like that,' he says slowly. 'You've really been alone, then. But that's not unusual.'

'I don't understand,' I say.

'Think about it a little,' he explains. 'What can you know of another man's heart? About what is really in his heart? How much do you know about your wife or your closest friend or your children? Then think of this: it's the same for everyone. Fundamentally no one gets to share their innermost thoughts and feelings. A rare few, perhaps, but I've never seen any.'

I see what he means, but only dimly.

'I want to tell you, Janardhanan, that you are just as alone as anyone else. That we are all the same.'

'All right,' I say, 'I understand. And so what, if I may ask?'

He thinks for a while, and his mouth works. This is a new habit of his, an old man's habit, and one that I hope I won't ever get. He says, 'Janardhanan, ever since we met that evening when you were troubled, I have been trying to console you. I am still trying to do that ... But that is not important. What is important is that I have been very foolish. There is no reason for me to console you. In effect, I must ask you to consider this an apology.'

'I do not understand this,' I say. 'How could somebody like you, educated and well-read, owe me an apology for wanting to console me?'

'Well-read I'll admit,' he says, 'but educated—I'm not sure. You place too much honour on book-learning. You know knots and ropes better than I ever will, as I know books better than you will. It's only a matter of exercising different parts of oneself, that's all. Don't think I am a better human being because I was a teacher and you a hangman. That is what the apology is for.'

'You owe me none, no matter what you have said or done.'

'So you say now, Janardhanan, but when you think about it you will see that I owe you one. And when you do see it, remember that I have already given it to you.'

Maash's apology stayed in my mind. I never asked him about it again. I remembered always the way his mouth worked soundlessly before he spoke. At the time it happened I thought it was one of the habits that he had acquired with age, but then I don't remember him doing that ever again. Apologizing to me must have been extremely painful for him, and I didn't want him to suffer that again. Maash was a friend.

~

The writer returned earlier than he said he would, in late May, and more than a week ahead of the date they said the monsoon rains would arrive.

He came alone early in the morning, before eight, and it was already warm. 'I hope you don't mind my coming at this time,' he said. 'Later in the day it will get very hot.'

'No problem,' I told him. 'I wake up at five and just waste my time.'

'Did you find the time to write while I was away?' he asked tentatively.

I laughed at his choice of words. Find the time, indeed! 'Yes, I wrote a little,' I replied. I handed him the book, the third now, and asked him to first read the part about Maash's apology. But I had made so many mistakes that he couldn't read it easily. He looked up at me uncomprehendingly, asked me the meanings of some of the longer Tamil words I'd used. 'I wish you'd brought the lady along,' I said.

'Yes. But why don't we look for someone nearby who knows Malayalam fairly well?' he asked.

So out we went, in search of a translator. I'd never

imagined that writing a book could involve so much work.

We found Murugan at his shop. Murugan is black and chubby and smiling, a good tradesman who stocks everything from needles to postage stamps. His shop is a sort of post office where people gather to gossip over tea or coffee. His customers include many Malayalis, and over the years of serving them coffee he has picked up their language as well. So we drank some coffee, and discussed the weather, and when there was a lull in his business, asked if he could translate for us.

He made himself a coffee and sat on the bench to a side of the counter, under the thatch awning. 'Tell me,' he said. I read out the tricky words and he translated them, explaining them to the writer in broken Malayalam. I don't know what the writer understood from his translation but he seemed happy and after settling with Murugan we went home. 'Do you understand his apology?' I asked.

'In a way, yes,' he replied.

I did not ask him to tell me. How would he understand Maash better than me? I knew what Maash meant, or felt I knew, and that was enough.

Now that the writer had returned, I felt a degree of calm. After he left that morning, I began seriously to look through what I had written in the notebooks. It seemed to be in no order: I had started where I wanted to, and gone along with the words as they came, without a direction, and when I read it I could see how disordered it was, how I leapt from topic to topic without any connection. I wondered how the writer was going to make sense of all this, and the blackness returned.

I sat with the notebooks for a while, and remembered a time when the blackness had grown almost overwhelming.

We have a king no more. I do not know what that means, and it has made no difference to me so far.

I am at my workplace, the prison. The main gate is open and, by daylight, ordinary. A tarred driveway stretches a hundred metres past the gate to a small traffic island, where it forks. Sparrows peck at the ground on the round traffic island, flying off when a vehicle passes by and settling down again when its wake has settled. The leftward path, which leads to the staff quarters, is blocked by a barrier manned by a policeman in khaki, while the right-hand path curves up along the side of a high wall and a ditch, leading into an old tile-roofed portico. The main door to the prison complex is to the left as you enter the portico. Above the door are these words, inscribed in white on a black stone set in the ochre wall: 'Central Prison, Poojapura. Opened by His Highness Ravi Vurma on September 23rd, 1886.'

Prince Ravi Varma, whose name, I gather, is misspelt on the stone, is long dead, and His Highness's descendants live in decaying splendour on the remnants of what was once a fabulous fortune. Even the old kingdom of Travancore is gone, sliced in two, divided between the two southernmost states of India, Tamil Nadu and Kerala. Only parts of the original prison remain: it has been altered and extended many times to accommodate far more prisoners than His Highness Ravi Varma would have imagined. But within the prison, unchanged for almost a century, is the scaffold where more than a thousand men have died at dawn.

I know that portico well, and the words on the stone. I had always thought that the kingdom was forever, and so was the king. Not that any king would last forever, but that there would always be a ruler from the dynasty, as there has been for the past two thousand years.

But now they tell me that the king has gone. They tell me further that the king was king at the pleasure of the queen of England and was himself ruled by the political resident in Trivandrum. They tell me that henceforth the king is purely a figurehead, and no different from a commoner. I do not understand this. How can one be the lord's representative on earth one day and a commoner—albeit a wealthy commoner—the next?

What I did I did in the name of the king, who I thought ordered it in the name of the lord. Eventually, therefore, I did my duty in the name of the lord. I was only an instrument of the lord, and that was my consolation for the act of taking from men what I cannot return to them.

Now that consolation is gone. Now I work for the government, not for the king. Now I discover that the king is not, and therefore never was, god come down to earth. What I have done in his name has not therefore been in the name of god.

How will I face god when my time comes?

~

Reading what I had written about the prison and the hangings, I was reminded of the other men who were there, besides the adiyaans.

Some people were regulars at hangings because their job demanded that they be present. One was the jail superintendent, who was in charge of the prison and one of the people who had to be present not only when the condemned man was hanged but also when he was certified dead. In the old days he was the one who played out the charade with the king's messenger. He was the one eventually responsible for the death of the condemned man, the one who gave the signal to the hangman to pull the lever.

Another was the doctor. There had to be one, usually the prison doctor. When he was away they would get one from the Medical College, or one in government service: an ordinary practitioner would not do. The doctor stayed after the body was cut down, did a quick autopsy to confirm how the prisoner died, and left as quickly as possible afterwards. These doctors were hardened to death but none wanted to stay in the confined space of the gallows enclosure.

A third was a judge. I don't know why a judge was necessary, but he was.

They came, stood around, watched the proceedings, and left.

These men aside, there were the other prison officials who were responsible for bringing the man from the condemned cell to the gallows enclosure. The rules said that the condemned man must be escorted to the gallows by a group of policemen led by an officer of the rank of sub-inspector or higher, and it was usual to have a group of a dozen warders doing the job, just in case the prisoner got violent. The warders were always unarmed.

And then there were the visitors. I remember occasions when the enclosure was full of people standing in the dew of early morning to see a hanging. I wonder why they came. Did they have something to do with the condemned man? Or any of his victims? One of the warders told me that the superintendent could permit people to watch the hanging, but only the privileged few got permission: high officials, politicians, and other influential people. Why would they want to see a hanging?

You might wonder how I came to know these things. In the dark of the mind that followed the departure of the king, and with him of the only consolation I had, I tried to find out as much as I could about hangings. I asked the warders about the rules. I had to ask again and again before they told me all this, but they told me in the end.

I must say, in passing, that not one of my friends ever asked if they could come to a hanging. They saw my state when I came back from a hanging and knew that it was not a sight to be seen, so they never asked. They were more sensitive to these matters than the privileged, perhaps, who had no qualms about watching death.

Of the others at the hangings, I remember some of the prison staff. Many of them kept their distance. Until the actual execution, until the moment I pulled the lever, until the moment when the process could no longer be reversed, they were outwardly respectful and tolerant. But when it was all over, they were in a hurry to get rid of me. When I had done what they could not, they threw me out, remembering me again only when they needed me next.

I remember the adiyaans at the temple by the school when my father killed the rooster with a single stroke of his broad-bladed knife. I remember their faces, and the mixture of contempt and respect there: it was exactly the same. This was also the treatment we got from the original aratchar family, the ones who kept the hangman's wealth and foisted the work off on us for a pittance.

I am troubled again.

I returned home the day before yesterday from a hanging. The prison staff paid me my allowances and seemed to be glad to get rid of me. I came back and had a drink or two, and slept. Today the lassitude that follows each hanging has passed and I am angry.

It was a bad hanging, for the man took a long time to die. As I was leaving the prison, I heard one of the jail staff, an officer, say to someone, purposely loud enough for me to hear, that I didn't know my job. I was tempted then to tell him that he could do it himself if he wished, but I held back.

So now I wait for Ramayyan to finish his evening prayer. I want to talk to him. I want to tell him what I heard in the prison, tell him that my anger does not leave me alone.

Ramayyan finds his peace in the rituals he does every day. I can see it in his eyes, his inward-looking eyes, as he emerges from the shrine. He signals me to sit, finishes his prayers, and joins me. He squats before me and asks, 'What is it?'

'Anger,' I tell him.

'What anger?' he asks.

I tell him. I tell him about the officer at the prison, and he listens very carefully. 'Shall I tell you something you might not like?' he says when I finish.

'Yes,' I tell him warily. Ramayyan is a quiet, diplomatic man, and even in the dusk I can see the peace shining in his eyes. He will say nothing untrue in this mood, and I will have to pay heed to him. I wonder if he's going to tell me that I really don't know my job.

'If you are a dog,' he says, 'and someone calls you a cat, who is the worse of the two of you? You, or the man who called you a cat?'

'The man who called me a cat. He's a fool.'

'He's a fool, he doesn't know the truth in front of him. Is it any use getting angry at a fool?'

'No ... Not really.'

'So if you are a dog and a man calls you a cat, you have no reason to be angry at him. Is that right?'

'I suppose so.'

'And if you are a dog, and a man calls you a dog, he's only telling the truth, isn't he?'

'Yes.'

'So if you're a dog, and a man calls you the dog, you have no reason to be angry at him, do you?'

'No … I suppose not.'

'So if a man says something about you, whether it's true or not, you should have no reason to get angry at him.'

'It's not like that, Ramayyan. We're not playing word games.'

'We're not playing games. All I'm telling you is this: if someone said you don't know your job, and you got angry at him, then you need to consider not what he said but the nature of your anger.'

I don't understand. I don't understand many of the things Ramayyan says, but this seems unfair. He has trapped me with words, and I cannot fight back because I have no learning. I would have said that all these words get in the way of real learning, but then Ramayyan seems to be genuine, he's not doing it to put me down. Then I see that I am angry at the prison official because his attitude seems to be exactly that of the members of the original aratchar family when we meet.

There is more than wordplay to what Ramayyan says. 'All right,' I tell him. 'We'll consider it. After that what?'

'Nothing,' he replies. 'Just think on it.'

'Is that what you do when you get angry?' I ask, a little upset, for he has told me nothing of any use.

'I try to do that,' he says, 'and sometimes my anger goes away. Sometimes it does not.'

'What do your holy books say?'

'Think about your anger. But they say two other things: one, that your anger hurts you most, not someone else; and two, that your anger doesn't matter.'

13

Again the words dried up. When the writer came next morning I complained to him. I told him I was troubled, and the man grinned, as if I had said something funny. 'What're you laughing at?' I asked him crossly.

'Your attack of writer's block,' he said. 'It's an occupational hazard.'

My irritation was growing by the second. 'I don't care what you call it,' I said. 'If you're any good as a writer you'd better tell me what I should do about it.'

'Okay,' he replied. 'Write about something that doesn't require too much thought. Write about something you know well.'

'Like what?' I asked, still angry.

'In all that you've written so far you haven't said anything about what you look like, or your wife, or your children. Or your father, for that matter. But start with yourself.'

'I can't do that,' I said, horrified. 'I can't describe myself. You do it. I described you, now you describe me.'

'You wanted to write the book,' he said, the grin emerging again.

'What will I write?' I detested the man's smugness sometimes.

'Describe yourself. Your vital statistics. Your height, weight, eye colour, skin colour, hair colour, hair length ...'

'That's no good!' I said. 'That's not enough!'

He laughed out loud. 'Exactly,' he said. 'Write about what you see in your eyes. What do the wrinkles on your face remind you of? Describe the man behind the features.'

~

The hangman has a ceremonial dress, black robes and a hood. He walks, ahead of the horse-cart, from his quarters in Kothuval Thirivu, next to Chalai police station, to the prison where the hanging will take place. In his robes, walking in the dark, lit only by the occasional street lamps along the road, followed by the jutka and behind that the drums, the melam and the chenda, he is a figure almost demonic.

Today in the king's house next to the police station I look in the mirror as I change into my 'uniform', and what I see is very commonplace. Behind the robes is a man, and an ordinary one at that. Look at him in daylight and you will see a man of average height for people of his ill-fed generation—five feet five inches or so. He is thin, slightly underweight, you would say, and the veins stand out in his forearms, which are visible, for he usually wears a bush-shirt, or no shirt. His hands are a size too large for the rest of him, his fingers are thick and his palms callused: there are a couple of marks there, rope burns that he has acquired over the years. His shoulders are square and his back straight, and his hard life has made him hardy and strong for his size and weight.

Normally he dresses in a colourful lungi which is folded up so that his legs are bare below the knees. In his house he is usually bare-chested, unless he has important visitors, and then he wears a bush-shirt with short sleeves. On occasions he wears a double-layered white mundu knotted about his waist, and a full-sleeved shirt, or a white jubba.

His hairline has receded a little but his hair is still thick, though it is greying fast. He wears it long, shoulder-length, unusual among men of his class because it takes a great deal of care and time to keep long hair from getting matted. He wears a beard, too, a long one, reaching down below the junction of his neck and his chest, and it is the same colour as his hair. His eyebrows, too, are pepper-and-salt, long and bushy under a forehead that looks broader than it is because of the receding hairline. On the forehead is a thick line of ceremonial ash from the temple: but this is for the occasion, for he usually wears a spot of sandal paste in the centre of his forehead. His nose juts forward, a sharp prow of a nose, with a flowing moustache underneath, and the cheekbones sticking out on either side: it is a gaunt face, the hangman's.

The eyes are dark brown, almost black, and deep-set, with lashes almost invisible. They are eyes dulled from the pressure of keeping thoughts in. Sometimes they are pained, and bear a hangdog look, but mostly they are neutral.

But the feet are different. They tell their own story. They are the broad feet of a man who has never worn shoes, and only rarely wears slippers. The toes are knobbly and the instep thick and veined, with the medium arch of a man who can walk long distances without effort. There is a hard carapace on the soles, again from walking long distances barefoot on bad surfaces: a small thorn won't penetrate this carapace. There are little scars all over the feet, from walking through thornbushes. The carapace helps when you have to clamber all over the scaffold.

I look at the feet anew and wonder where they have been. Then I remember, my father's feet looked the same. No wonder, for I travel the route he did.

~

While I might have done a hundred-odd hangings, the gallows on which I did them must have seen over a thousand since 1886, when the prison was built. Hangings were far more frequent in the old days.

What would the gallows be like now? There were a few more hangings after I left, the last I heard of being in the late seventies—I forget which year. Must have been about fifteen years ago: I remember it vaguely because it was the year one of my grandchildren was born.

A thousand hangings would have left their mark on the gallows, as a hundred have left their mark on me. The night after I thought about this, I had a dream. I remember it only vaguely. I dreamt of going for a hanging, of going around the gallows enclosure checking the pillars and just looking around, and I remember thinking in the dream that it was strange, my being there at that time, because the sun was up and in the east, and I never went there for a hanging except when the sun was in the west or not up at all …

The prison wall forms a rough circle, with the bell tower in the centre dominating the enclosure.

When you enter the porch there is a staircase leading upwards, to the superintendent's office. But past the porch is the entrance into the prison proper, a primer-coated metal door with a judas door built into it, guarded by at least two warders. Anyone who enters must sign in here. Inside you see another wall, running right around the prison, just like the outer wall.

If you consider the prison as a clock face, with the entrance at six o'clock, the prison hospital is at twelve o'clock, diametrically opposite the entrance, a low tile-roofed building where a doctor is always on duty. To a side of the hospital, at about eleven o'clock, is another complex that houses undertrials: unlike convicted prisoners, undertrials do not work during the day. The mess where the prisoners are brought in to eat at half-past noon is at four o'clock, within the inner wall. Between the inner wall and the outer, close to the hospital, spread out between twelve o'clock and nine o'clock, are a temple, a mosque, and a church.

The gallows is at five o'clock, in an enclosure, the outer wall of which is the outer wall of the prison: about twenty metres of it. It is roughly triangular, with two doors. The smaller of the two doors, about four feet high, is set in the outer wall: this is the door through which the body of the condemned man is handed over to whoever has come to collect it. The larger door is the way the man is brought into the gallows enclosure from the condemned cell.

The gallows is set in a concrete platform that is raised a foot or so off the ground. The condemned man must descend a few steps as he enters the enclosure, walk a few yards, and climb three steps on to this platform. In the centre of this platform is the trapdoor, which is a little over three feet long and two feet broad. It is made of thick teak planks, held together by iron strips that run along its breadth.

At the corners of the rectangular platform are four poles that support a peaked roof of corrugated asbestos. It was a regular tiled roof in the old days, but some years ago they changed it. In a corner of the enclosure, not far from the little door through which the body goes, is a small concrete pillar that used to support a water tap that is no longer there. The tap served a purpose once;

it was used to wash the dead man's body sometimes. No one does that anymore.

Straddling the trapdoor stand two pillars of teak. To the side of one of the pillars is the handle that operates the trapdoor, and on that pillar, about four feet up, is a hook where one end of the rope will be knotted. The pillars are blackened with age, but well-seasoned and strong, and across their tops lies a beam, also six inches to a side. This beam can support a huge weight, but the most it will need to support is one-and-a-half times the weight of the heaviest man likely to be hanged on it—this when the large stone is used to test the rope a day before a hanging.

On the upper surface of the crossbeam, placed in its centre, a little over an inch apart, are two little iron spikes that stick out about two inches. The rope, when it is placed to kill a man, passes between these two spikes. At the side of one of the pillars are set two-inch triangles of teak, small steps that offer a man a toehold while he climbs up the pillar to pass the rope between the spikes.

Finding the spot where the rope passes is easy. A thousand hangings and more have worn two grooves on the crossbeam, one between the two spikes, where the rope passes when a man is being hanged, and another groove to a side, where the rope passes when it is being tested.

A few points to remember: one, that when the rope is being tested, the weight used is at least one-and-a-half times the weight of the condemned man;

and two, that for each hanging, three ropes are tested. You would expect the groove worn by the testing to be deeper: the rope is tested thrice each time, and with a much greater weight. But it isn't. It's the other groove, the one between the spikes, the one worn by a thousand men at the end of a rope, that is deeper, and it is far deeper. The reason is this: when the rope is being tested, the trapdoor opens and the stone falls, the rope jerks at the end of the fall, and then the stone hangs motionless until it is taken down; but when a man falls he sometimes struggles for minutes at the end of the rope.

The final struggles of a thousand dying men have worn that deep groove in the dark, seasoned teak of the crossbeam.

I remembered those grooves, sitting under a tree a quarter-century after my last hanging. I hadn't noticed them when I used to go regularly to the gallows, and I don't understand how then the memory could have stayed in my mind. For a moment I considered asking the writer if he knew anything of the nature of such memories, if he knew how to dig them out of the mind. But I did not. I did not ask because I knew he would give me a little lecture on how those memories were formed and tell me a few fancy new words in English to describe them: in what he said there would be nothing of value to an old man trying to write a book for the first time in his life. That man is full of long words and surprises. I suppose he could be a good man if he tried hard, but he'd have to try very hard.

I would find the memories myself, however imperfectly.

~

The condemned man is led out of his cell at four in the morning.

The previous night he was fed what he wanted. Within limits, he can eat what he wishes for his last supper. There is a custom here that the condemned man eats what the jail superintendent eats. It started when one of the superintendents, one Raghavan Nair, an honest man, asked a condemned man, 'What would you like for your last meal?'

The prisoner replied, addressing the superintendent as yejuman, meaning master, 'I would like to eat what the yejuman eats tonight.'

Raghavan Nair, being somewhat considerate, went home and asked his wife to cook a little more than usual, as if to feed a guest, and sent a portion to the prison. This practice caught on, until there came a time when the jail superintendent got a little allowance for feeding the condemned man one meal from his own table.

The chances are that the condemned man sleeps little. The condemned cell, where he has spent perhaps a year or more—in recent times two years or more, while his sentence goes through the appeal process—is as brightly lit through the night as the rest of the prison, and there is a man on watch throughout, a warder who can look into the cell through the simple barred door.

He must bathe before the hanging, and he is offered hot water, if he desires it, which some do, especially in the mild winters. After his bath he puts on a fresh uniform, a clean white uniform these days, unlike the old striped uniform, and then he is led out of the enclosure which holds the condemned cell, past the door with the peephole, to the passage between the walls enclosing prisoner wards A and B. He walks along the packed earth passage in slippers, if he has any, or on bare feet.

Short of the exit from the prison he turns left. Another few yards, and the door to the gallows enclosure is to his right. There he turns, stooping automatically to avoid hitting his head on top of the doorway, and walks down the steps, down the path trodden through the grass by a thousand pairs of condemned feet, up the steps to the platform, and on to the darker patch in the centre of the trapdoor: that is his last step.

The warders with him make final adjustments in his position before his arms are tied behind him. Then his legs are tied, at the ankles and the knees, and finally the mask goes on his face. The noose, which is already prepared, I place about his neck, and tighten, so the knot falls beneath and behind the right ear, as I have been taught.

When everything is ready, and everyone is ready, the superintendent looks at his watch to check that the time is right. When he gives the signal, I tug hard at the lever that operates the trapdoor, and the man who was standing in the centre of the platform disappears. The only trace of him is the quivering of the rope, which sometimes lasts for a few minutes.

My work is done. The body will be cut down later, and death certified by the doctor observing the hanging. The time and cause of death will be noted, and an entry made in the prison's log. Then the body will be handed over to relatives, if there are any willing to take it: if not, it is sent off to the crematorium where it will be converted into ashes and fragments of bone.

I walk away. There is a little paperwork to be done, and I sign a voucher for the cash that the superintendent pays me: my allowance for coming to finish off the man.

The next time I come, the first thing I will see when I enter the gallows enclosure will be the dark spot worn in the centre of the trapdoor made of stained old planks, the spot to which a thousand pairs of feet have taken their last step. In my mind that spot is very clearly visible, for there are the marks of feet all the way up to it, but none leading away.

14

The rains came, in their plenty. There was water in the canal after the first heavy rain of the year, and in a week some of the low-lying areas were flooded. The path to my house became a strip of wet mud, and if you walked in it wearing slippers you had your rear splashed with drops of dirty water thrown up by your heels. The water from the first couple of rains disappeared quickly into the fields, leaving behind a coolness and the fragrance of newly-wet earth. All around there was new life in the air, and in the sown fields there was rejoicing.

When it rained the sparrows and mynahs and stray dogs cowered in whatever shelter they could find, and when it stopped they emerged, shaking the water off their bodies, looking for food that was easy to find. After the long hot summer when hunger drove them far afield in their hunt for food, the rains made a great change for the birds.

But not for me. After writing about the trapdoor and the grooves on the crosspiece I slept badly for a few nights, and occasionally I flared up at Chellammal. I thought about it, even asked the writer about why it was happening, but he spoke his usual empty words and left me to face my sleepless nights alone.

I went walking in the mud, caught a fever, and went to bed. The writer came and offered to take me to the doctor. 'This happens every year when I am careless,' I told him. 'It's not worthwhile.'

'As you wish,' he said. 'But don't write while you're sick.'

'Don't be stupid,' I told him. 'How can I write lying in the dark?'

'Don't think too much about it.'

'Don't be stupid,' I repeated. 'How can I help thinking about it, lying in the dark, doing nothing?'

The fever passed in three days and when I was well I told him I was going for a walk, and he came along. I think he came along to make sure that I did nothing foolish: he forgot that I was twice his age and twice as capable of taking care of myself. During some of those chats, during walks armed with umbrellas to keep the rain off our heads, he asked me some questions that I told him I was not going to answer. 'Why not?' he asked.

'I ask you why I don't get to sleep properly after I write something and you don't tell me anything of use,' I snapped. Then I thought I had been unnecessarily harsh on him. He was, after all, doing his best.

And so, one morning, when the sun came briefly out, I decided to write down some of those questions and my answers. They were good questions, some of them, and since I couldn't proceed with my writing I thought I would try to answer them as best I could. This was a journal, after all, and I could put in it whatever went through my mind.

'What is it like to kill a man in cold blood?' he had asked once. That's very hard to answer, because when I used to do it for a living I used to tell myself that after you've done it a few times you stop noticing it. You forget. But that's not true. Killing a man is like closing a door forever, and when you do it you lose a part of yourself forever.

'What do you see when you look in his eyes?' he had asked, looking me in the eye. One thing I always feared I would see but never actually saw was blame. No condemned man ever looked at me with accusation in his eyes. The warders told me that sometimes they got to know the condemned man well: after all, he did spend a year or two in their custody, and in that period they saw him regularly. Even the warders said that when they led the man to the gallows, there was no accusation in his eyes, which were usually turned inwards. But I always feared to look the condemned man in the eye: what if his eyes were turned outwards?

'Was there a link between you and the condemned man?' Yes, I would answer this question, there was. At the time I put the noose about the man's neck I would tell him silently that I did it in the name of the king, and of dharma, and not of my own volition. Though he heard me not, I asked his pardon then, knowing that it would be granted if he had thought about his deeds during the long wait for his final sentencing.

'What did you see in the eyes of people around you after you had hanged your man?' I saw relief, and I saw contempt. I saw the contempt sometimes of a man too weak to do his own dirty work, who could afford to have someone else do it for him. I saw them shutting themselves off from me … I found this painful.

'Did you look at the body as it hung in the well under the trapdoor?' In the old days I had to. I had to go down into the well in the dark and watch the body being cut down. I had to take a piece of the rope, and then I walked away up the stairs towards the light. Each time I did that I hoped I would never have to do it again.

'Where would you look at the moment you pulled the lever?' At the lever itself. Where else could I look? Silly question. Or perhaps it's not so silly.

'Do you fear his relatives?' No. I used to, but no longer. I fear no one now, not even my old friend, Death Himself, for He has come close by over a hundred times. But perhaps I fear what I myself have done …

When I got as far as this I saw something else in my mind's eye: the quivering of a rope on a rainy morning when you could see the rope only because it quivered.

The condemned man is on the trapdoor. His face is masked and his hands are tied behind him but he is tense; standing close by, I can see it in the quick rise and fall of his shoulders as he breathes deeply, and in the quiver in his fingers behind him.

The sun is up: the superintendent's orders are to execute the man as early as possible after sunrise. Any time now. I look over the condemned man: check that the knot is in the right place, beneath the right ear; check the knots at his wrists and ankles; check the mask; give the lever a little shake, to check if it will move smoothly after yesterday's oiling. Everything is in place. All I need is the signal to go ahead.

The superintendent nods, and the time has come. The lever tends to stick a bit so you have to give it a good firm tug: I am glad that the lever takes my attention at this time. I tug the lever, and it moves jerkily towards me, like a gear change lever in an old bus. Then there is the thump of the trapdoor hitting the pillar on the far side, and the man disappears.

In the instant I pull the lever the man has disappeared. The people watching react differently. The prison staff, who are used to this, tend to avert their eyes. My own eyes sweep around the small enclosure. There are raincoats all over, and a few umbrellas. All the faces in the enclosure have changed in that little instant, and in the vast majority of them I see relief. But their eyes are still caught by something, for they stand still and stare. I look at what they are watching, and I see the rope quivering.

It goes on and on and on. God, how it goes on!

I, too, stare with the rest.

From below come the sounds of the man voiding himself: his bladder first, then his bowels. I shrink from those faint sounds, and from the faint stench that floats up through the open trapdoor. The wet breeze blows the smell up to me and the others, and it hangs in the air for a while before a gust of wind blows it away. As I get a whiff of it I can't help thinking that the prisoner's last bath was useless. The purpose of allowing him to bathe is to avoid having to clean the body afterwards. But there is no one to clean up the body: the dead man's relatives will have to do it themselves, a final indignity.

At long, long, last, the quivering stops. The man is dead.

To me it lasted hours. Later they tell me it was over in minutes.

Here it is, my own guilt. Have I done my job well?

People say that the hangman's job is an art. Positioning the knot under the prisoner's ear is the most important part of the job: get it exactly right and there's not a quiver from the rope except for that little jerk at the drop, when his neck breaks. A few millimetres off, and the man's neck doesn't break: he dies of strangulation, slowly, painfully.

That's what has happened this time. My 'art' failed me. God knows it's not an art, and I'm not an artist. No one ever taught me how to get it exactly right. No one has ever come back to me and said, 'Hey, the last time you tied your knot it hurt, tie it a little more to the right.'

So where does a hangman learn his art?

I don't know where other hangmen learnt it, but I got it in a few lessons from my father, when I accompanied him. Raman accompanied him many more times. Raman came with me a few times after Father was gone, and showed me what he had learnt from Father. But he had learnt little, I know. Was it that Father, too, didn't know? How do hangmen learn except by being shown each thing? And how does one show another where to tie the knot and how, and explain how to choose the spot? How can they expect the hangman to know? Some of these people are better educated, more widely travelled, and yet they expect the hangman to know.

Maybe Raman would have made a better hangman, but he refused. Maybe he was the braver of the two of us.

God, I should have refused, too. When I see the rope quiver like this, I wish I had refused too.

Forgive me for not refusing. I did it to feed my children.

15

The sun was gone behind dark grey rain-clouds brooding in the sky. The humidity lay heavy in the air, and the breeze carried spray from far away. It was about five in the evening, I knew instinctively, for Chellammal had just taken away the empty tumbler from which I had had my coffee. A drizzle started, and droplets plinked in the puddles on the ground. From above came raindrops, falling off the leaves heavily with a strange regularity. My hair was wet, and soon Chellammal came out of the house, screaming something. 'What?' I asked, for I didn't understand what she said.

'Have you been sitting in the rain all this while?' she asked. 'Have you forgotten that you just got over the fever?'

The notebook was damp. The ink hadn't blotched, because the pen was good. I didn't want the book to get any wetter, so I picked it up and carried it in. On the way I sneezed, and Chellammal brought me a towel to wipe my head. The power had gone off and inside the house it was dark, though the kerosene lamp was lit. I was tired and I lay down to rest on one of the two cots. The weariness was not in my body but in my mind. I had discovered something, but the discovery had brought pain, not joy.

When I wrote about the quivering of the rope I knew the source of at least some of the blackness. Writing was the easy part; living with what you learnt while writing was difficult.

Amidst the rains and the fresh life blooming all around I found the blackness now firmly in place. It sat on my shoulder like an old grey ghost that wouldn't let go no matter what I did. I wished I had never started on this book. I wished I had sent the writer and his interpreter away when they came, pretended that I knew nothing of the aratchar. It would have been so easy.

All things would have been easy. They would have been easier still if half a century or more ago I had found the sense to tell my father firmly that I, like his eldest son, would never be a hangman. Would he have understood, I thought uselessly. His father hadn't been a hangman, and in his childhood he must have known hunger. He must have said it from the best motives, despite knowing what it was like to be a hangman.

He must have known. Why did he not tell me?

Did he suffer the blackness as I do?

That night I had the old dream again. But this time it was different, and even more frightening.

I see the steps first, the irregular stone steps leading into the dark well below the trapdoor, but now they are clearer than they used to be. I can see the joints in the stones, and a few rough patches on the steps at the top. All around is the soft darkness before the dawn, but there are no stars in the sky above: there is only blackness. There is light from the powerful lamps in the tower, but they seem not to work everywhere: I can see the grass on the ground, and the moisture at the top of the steps, but further away it is all dark.

From far away comes the sound of drums, rising and falling. I feel the chill wind on my cheek. The drums are very faint, and I do not know if they are really drums or just some faraway noise.

In the darkness of the well lurks the old menace, the one I cannot name. I stand on the uppermost step of the staircase and look down, and see a flicker of movement below, but it is gone as I see it. I turn from the well to look for my adiyaans, who accompanied me into the enclosure.

They are still there, with the guards and the masked man. But even as I watch, they disappear, and I am confused: did I come alone?

For a fleeting moment I see the reassuring figure of Maash ... But in a moment he too is gone.

Now I am alone, I think. But I am not. There's the man in the mask, standing on the trapdoor, with the noose above him. In his crisp, striped uniform he stands very still. In this dream too the rope is a clean bright white that seems to glow on its own. And again I see that the knots at his ankles are neatly tied. His arms are tied behind him.

I have a memory of having tied many knots.

My adiyaans are gone. In their place stand men with masks. Men with nooses about their necks, men in the familiar uniform.

There is something strange about all those masks. The beat of the faraway drums rises, and I see that the masks are all too flat.

And then there is only one man in a mask.

The mask is the face. It is a hundred and seventeen faces.

The terror rises. I have to get away, but I cannot run, there is no escape.

The iron door to the gallows enclosure, I know, is less than thirty feet away, but it takes an age and all my strength to reach it. It is locked with a massive padlock. Moving painfully, I get to the only other door, the small one through which they pass the body to relatives waiting outside, but on that too is a similar padlock. There are walls around me, twice as high as me and completely smooth. There is no escape.

Something makes me turn around despite myself, and I see the man in the flat mask, his arms and legs free. How did he free himself from the knots I myself put about his wrists and ankles? The ropes must have fallen off somehow. Then I look at the mask and see the eyes. The eyes are bright: they are full of a light that is baleful and derisive. They are so bright I cannot look in them anymore.

His hands tighten about my neck. They are powerful, cold hands, I cannot pry them loose. They tighten further, and I cannot breathe ... I try to close my eyes and shut out the burning eyes but I cannot. I begin to sink to my knees and my heart threatens to burst in my chest.

And then I wake up, gasping for breath, with my eyes closed tight.

When I came awake I was cold, and shivering under the thin sheet with which I had covered myself. A bumblebee hummed in a corner and water plick-plocked down from a leak in the roof. From outside came the patter of a gentle drizzle, and the sough of the breeze in the trees. The windows were all closed: Chellammal must have shut them to keep the cold out. It was stifling inside the house. I wanted to open a window, but felt too weak to do so.

When the thirst became too powerful, I rose slowly, but Chellammal sleeping close by was alert. 'What is it?' she asked, sitting up.

'Water,' I said. 'I'm thirsty.'

'You're not well,' she grumbled softly. 'How could you be so silly as to sit in the rain all afternoon?'

'Shut up and get me the water,' I told her, 'we will talk about this in the morning.'

'Send that man away,' she said as she brought me the pot of water and a tumbler.

'What man?' I asked after I had taken a long gulp. I knew whom she meant.

'The writer. The one who gave you those books.' There was a faint edge of desperation in her voice. 'You've been different ever since he came.'

Sitting in the dark in the wee hours of a wet and windy morning, in a house full of stale air and traces of smoke, I had perhaps my most intimate conversation with Chellammal in twenty years, maybe more. 'Different how?'

'Changed ... Unpredictable. Not like before.'

'What was I before?'

'You were quiet, you had your regular habits ... Now you don't ... You just sit in the backyard and when I come there you don't even see me. The way you talk is different, and sometimes you don't listen to me. You seem to be far away, beyond reach of the rest of us.'

'But I'm here. I don't do anything strange. I got drunk once, but that was only once ... in all these months. I haven't had any since.'

'It's not what you do. It's how you do it.'

'How do I do all these things?'

'I am not educated ... Why do you ask me these things? I cannot explain.'

'Sleep, then, I am the same. Don't worry.' I lay back, and I heard her settle down again. The minutes passed, and her breathing deepened until she began to snore.

Sleep did not come to me. First I blamed it on the closeness in the room, and opened a window to let in some fresh air. That brought insects, and I lay awake scratching at bites. But I knew that I wouldn't be able to sleep anyway, insects or not, closeness or not.

I knew then that Maash had seen this coming. So, perhaps, had Ramayyan Gurukkal. The gurukkal's advice was more roundabout, for he would quote from his scriptures in Sanskrit. At the time I used to wonder why those two men were wasting their time and mine telling me something I did not understand and could not use, but as I lay awake I knew that it was not a waste of time. There was something there for me to think about.

~

I have known all along of the Bhagavad Gita, the song of god, but nothing about what is in it. To me it is just a string of words in a language I do not know. It is not for the likes of me to claim knowledge of the Gita.

It is dusk on a February evening: at six, it is already too dark to read. I am at Ramayyan's temple, waiting, though I am not quite sure what I wait for. This morning the summons came, that there will be a hanging in Poojapura eight days from now, and I have come here to meet Ramayyan and fix up a puja for tomorrow morning. There will be another, of course, on the morning I leave, but tomorrow's will be the first.

The summons always comes a few days before the hanging. It comes by mail, usually, and when I see those long brown envelopes with the stamped message saying 'On Government Service' I know they can be nothing else. The day the summons arrives I go to the temple, where I ask Ramayyan Gurukkal to do a puja for me. The days that remain until I go off to test the gallows at Poojapura pass slowly. The moments trudge heavily past, and I wish vaguely for some release, for another life.

Waiting for Ramayyan to finish his evening prayers, I am reminded of the first summons I got, before

Independence. In those days the summons would come not by post but in the hands of a royal messenger. I wondered why the king bothered to send a messenger all the way when there was a perfectly usable postal system. I realized only much later how the system worked. The king wanted to ensure his aratchar's loyalty. He didn't want to pay too much, so he made the hangman's job look a privileged one. Hence the messenger, so that the people around would know that the hangman was close to the king himself.

The king didn't mind his original appointees handing over the job—not the income, of course, only the dirty work—to poor relatives. He wouldn't have cared very much, for the hangman's right was assigned to the clan and not to any particular person. The messenger always went to the house of the original aratchar family, at Bimaneri, some dozen kilometres from my house in Parvathipuram. From there the others sent word: There will be a hanging ... Now, since Independence, the king's laws do not work, and the government sends me sealed envelopes with my name on them . . .

All this runs through my mind as Ramayyan completes his prayers. He has two shrines here, two altars, one where the sacrifice is a goat, and the other where it's a rooster, where I do the sacrifice. I have never seen a goat being sacrificed—I don't think Ramayyan has done it in recent years—and have never asked what it is for. Perhaps Ramayyan will tell me someday.

He emerges from the shrine with a small bunch of red flowers clutched to his breast. His eyes are open but he does not see in front of him: he is guided by habit, and his mind is still on his prayers. I wait for him to put the flowers away on a small square of banana leaf, make a last bow to the deity, and get out into the compound. There he takes a deep breath before he sees me. 'A puja tomorrow?' he asks. 'The usual?'

'Yes,' I tell him.

'I'll do it,' he says. He turns to look at a bird returning to nest in a jackfruit tree in a corner of his small compound. 'What is it? You look as if you want to ask me something.'

'Yes,' I tell him. 'This is not a good time, the time I spend waiting ... What can I do?'

He looks at me, without curiosity. 'Don't we spend most of our lives waiting? Waiting for something to happen, then waiting for something else, and then waiting to die? You do your duty as best you can, and leave the rest to god.'

'Is that what you do?' I ask.

He smiles. 'No. That is what I would like to do. That is what it says in my holy book, the Gita.'

'Does your book talk about the difficulty of waiting?'

'It doesn't talk of waiting. It just talks of doing your work without thinking of what will come of it.'

'But how can you do something and not think of what will come of it? Will a farmer sow seeds and not wait for the rains?'

'A farmer has to sow the seeds at the right time, whether or not the rains come. What matters is not what he does but how he does it.'

'He has to sow the seeds, but what does he do after that but wait for the rain? And while he is waiting, will he not worry?'

'His worrying will not help. It will make no difference to the rains.'

'It's impossible not to wait watchfully when your children might starve.'

'All that the book says is, while you're waiting, wait. Your worry won't feed your children. Your actions might.'

'Actions. Does the book tell you what to do?'

'All it says is, do your dharma.'

'And what is my dharma, does it say?'

'No. That is for you to say.'

'But it's because I don't know what I should do that I ask you if there is anything in the scriptures.'

'I understand. But your dharma is your own.'

'All I can say is, I don't understand your book. And perhaps your book doesn't understand people like me.'

Ramayyan smiles. 'Leave it. I know how you feel. I too have children.'

'Yes,' I tell him. 'I will be here tomorrow. With the rooster.'

So the scriptures offered nothing. Ramayyan at the time seemed to be speaking nonsense, for I went to him to know what to do, and he said that the scriptures avoided just that question. So where did this whole thing of dharma come from?

I wondered about it after I got back, but the thinking didn't last under the pressures of family life. When you have a wife and several children living in a two-room house it's difficult to take care of all of them and have time to think about why you do what you do. Throughout the period of waiting I immersed myself in family life. I spent time with my children, and when I could I worked in the fields.

The nights were the worst, though, for I did not sleep well. On normal days I would go to bed with Chellammal, and after we joined, sleep came quickly. But on these nights I could not make love to Chellammal, or I would lie sleepless afterwards, after the unsatisfactory coupling that left both of us with a distaste for it. And sex was something I enjoyed, and so did Chellammal. We did, after all, have nine children over a period of about twenty years. That is something I have never regretted: one of the regrets of my old age is that my vigour is gone.

So those sleepless nights during the period of waiting stay in my memory. Sleepless sweaty nights when the seconds crawled by, leaving a weight in my heart.

When I think back, I think of what Ramayyan told me, about doing my duty. What was my duty?

I didn't know then, and I don't know still. Was it my duty to be a hangman?

I have no answer to that, but I do know that even if it was, I failed in my duty.

Though I realize this only now, almost forty years later. The night after I returned from Ramayyan's temple, wondering what my dharma was, I kept seeing the quivering rope from that rainy day. I remembered the man at the end of the rope emptying his bowels. I remembered the faint stench. The memory troubled me all night, each night till the day of the hanging. I suffered but without comprehension. If someone had asked me then why that memory haunted me, I would have had no answer, for I did not understand. Now I do.

My duty was to make sure that every condemned man died as painlessly as possible. If I had known exactly where to place the knot, since that is what makes the difference, I would have done my duty. I did not do that. I failed completely; I caused pain. Now I think, I could have asked the prison doctor about it: he would have known how the man died, he would have known how a man should die when hanged. But I never did that. I was lost to the myth of the art of the hangman, and as a result people suffered in their last moments at my hand. No wonder sleep came hard.

After I finished this passage I felt drained, and there was a dry, bitter taste in my mouth. For the first time in my life I said to myself that it would be easy to die.

16

In the morning I came half awake late to the sounds of Chellammal washing and cooking in our small, dark kitchen.

They are reassuring, these sounds, when a man is ill. The clink of the water pot, the whistling hiss of Chellammal blowing through a small cardboard tube to get the fire going, and the hiss and crackle of the fire itself, the muted conversation and deliberate footsteps.

Outside it was still dark. In the rains, when the clouds are thick, dawn passes without our knowing it. Even the rooster sleeps late, and truly there is no need to be up and about early, for there is no livestock to be tended, no cows to be milked before the dawn. I turned over and grunted in my dim contentment, wishing to sleep a little longer.

Then Chellammal dropped a pot with a clang, and that woke me up. I sat up with the memory of the old nightmare in my mind and that awful bitter taste in my mouth. My anger rose. Why couldn't she be a little more careful in the morning? 'Can't you take care of your pots and pans?' I asked as she bent to pick up the pot, the sarcasm sharp in my voice. 'Or did you perhaps think it was time I got out of bed?'

'It slipped from my hands in the dark,' she replied. 'And if I wanted to wake you up I would have poured its contents over your face.'

'Careful what you say,' I said.

'Easy for you to talk. All you have to do is lie around and eat and talk, when you're not in the backyard with your useless book or out chatting with your useless friends.'

'My friends are none of your business,' I thought of Maash, then, with his shrew of a wife, with her loud high voice and cutting words.

She put the pot down and turned to face me, her hands on her hips. 'When your friends get you drunk and keep you away from home all night, they are my business. When they come and give you dangerous ideas and tempt you to sit in the backyard scribbling and watching the grass grow, they are my business ...' She glared at me, challenging me to respond.

My thought of the night returned, that it would be easy to die, and if I died, none of this would matter. I got up and went looking for a neem twig to brush my teeth with. Despite our little shouting match Chellammal had my coffee ready, and soon after that my breakfast. I ate my idlis hot, and picked up my old umbrella to keep me company while I walked. 'Where are you going?' she asked when she saw me pick up the umbrella.

'Out,' I said. 'For a walk.'

She turned her back to me but I knew she was angry still. And, to my own surprise, I found I didn't really care.

It had begun to rain again. I found a small, quiet lane to walk in, for it was impossible to walk in the fields, and there was too much traffic on the main road.

Maash has not come this way for a few days, and I have been missing him. It is unlike him to miss a walk, and if his wife had been a little more tolerant I would have gone to his house to ask about him.

When I do see him, it is on a rainy evening, and he has his umbrella in his hand, a big old one with a worn, curved handle. We walk in silence for a while, the rain a steady drumbeat on our umbrellas, our feet squelching in puddles on the roadside. We have to hold the umbrellas low to keep the rain and the spray off our faces, so we can only see the ground a few paces ahead. We do not see the faces of passers-by, and it's only when the noise of an engine warns us that we watch out for vehicles.

Maash is preoccupied with something. He walks much faster than usual, at a pace that for a man his age is furious. We take a side road, a narrow lane where at this time of the evening there is no traffic. It is a wealthy part of town, not far from Kanya Milk

Factory, and the wealth and power of the people in these parts show.

Nearly two kilometres into the walk, we pass under a banyan, an old banyan with foliage thick enough to keep the rain off, and in that moment's freedom from the rain he looks up and pauses. He looks at his watch, and waits for a moment to catch his breath. 'I've been hurrying,' he says. 'Sorry.' He is wheezing a little.

'It doesn't matter,' I tell him. 'I'm used to it, and I'm much younger than you are.' I wait for a cyclist to pass. 'I was concerned that you might be exhausted.'

He looks at me from under his bushy eyebrows, which are now almost white, and smiles. 'Janardhanan, we have known each other all these years, and you know what my home life is like.'

'Yes,' I reply, 'I know.'

'You once followed me home, didn't you?' he asks.

'Yes,' I reply, surprised.

'I know you did, someone told me that a man with your beard and nose had followed me one evening. It could only be you.'

I stumble for an explanation. 'I was only ...'

He raises a hand to silence me. 'Janardhanan, how many children do you have?'

'Nine,' I reply, surprised again at this change of subject.

'How are they doing?'

I don't know what to say. They are all literate. The boys are not too badly off: one has a clerical job in Calicut, one is a mechanic with a government transport company in Madras, and the third ... The third is not very educated, but he gets by with odd jobs. The girls ... I have six daughters, and sometimes I think I failed them, for none of them has had a really good marriage. They are all still with their respective husbands, but I have felt sometimes the curse of being a hangman when I think of them. 'Some are doing well, and the rest just survive,' I reply, as honestly as I can.

'Do they visit you once in a while?'

'The boys come regularly. My daughters come when they can, with the grandchildren.'

'And when they come, what do you do?'

'Nothing. We talk. I spend time with the grandchildren when I can.'

'Do you know how fortunate you are, Janardhanan? I have three daughters. They are all at home now, and I am tired of them.' There is nothing for me to say, so I wait for him to continue. 'Do you know why I haven't come this way these past few days? All my daughters are like their mother ... I don't know what to do, Janardhanan. I have been leaving my house earlier these days, and taking a different route ... They drive me away from my house, and they speak of me with contempt to their children. Where did I fail?'

The anguish is plain in his voice. We walk in silence for a while, and he recovers himself. 'I have always liked to learn, from anywhere, from anyone. You know that I belong to a high caste, and that I don't care about it. But she does, and she has taught the children to care about it. Stupid woman. I should have left her long ago.'

A little further, his voice begins to change: it steadies out. The anguish is receding, and he is becoming pensive. 'It's all right,' he says. 'I don't really mind. Most of the time it doesn't bother me, but today I'm upset because I overheard my own daughter telling her son not to listen to me, that I don't know what I'm doing.'

'How can it be all right?' I blurt.

'It's as much my fault as theirs,' he says. 'I could have been rich and I refused. I could have given them much more than I have, and I didn't. They hold it against me because I did what I liked ... I wanted to read and teach and learn, and I did just that. I didn't care to listen to my wife's entreaties.' He pauses again. 'Janardhanan, when you pursue something single-mindedly, you stand to lose a lot. If you want to be really good at anything, you have to be willing to lose something. I don't know if I'm any good at what I do, but it has cost me peace in my later life, as you can see. But it has still been worthwhile. All these other things, they are only pinpricks. Just do what you have to do.'

I don't understand what he means, but today I will not ask him. I will listen quietly to whatever he says, and I will keep it to myself. I am proud again that he has chosen to confide in me, and hope that someday I will understand him.

~

It was pouring outside; I could no longer sit in the backyard with my notebook. I was sitting inside the house, under the naked bulb hanging from the ceiling, straining to write. My own shadow fell over the book, and no matter how I tried, I couldn't find a position where the light was bright and my shadow didn't fall over the page. So I gave up trying and put my elbows on the table and prepared for some eyestrain.

It was on just such a day of rain, twenty years ago, that Maash had talked about loss in the pursuit of learning. And at last I knew what he meant then. When I thought of Chellammal's angry face, and her back, stiff with resentment, I knew what Maash meant. And when I looked in my own mind, and my own lack of reaction to Chellammal's anger, I knew what he meant when he said that his wife's behaviour didn't bother him.

What mattered to me was my own guilt, and finding out what I could do about it. If I had done something wrong, there must be something I could do to atone for it. I could not imagine a god who would not permit atonement. I cursed the writer briefly for bursting into my life with his misplaced youthful enthusiasm and waking the ghosts in my head. But the ghosts were always there anyway. They haunted my sleep. Perhaps I would sleep better now that they haunted my waking hours.

17

What had I lost?

Had I lost something when I agreed to become a hangman? I did it to keep the family going, and I didn't lose the family. My wife lives with me, and I have reason to believe that she is not terribly unhappy with her life. My children are all grown up and gone away, and though my daughters have not married as well as I would have liked them to, I have no great reason to complain.

Is this what I haven't lost? Is this what I have gained out of my failure to refuse the hangman's job? I think of Raman when I consider this, Raman, my brother, who had to leave home and work far away. I wonder, was he any happier there?

The more I think of it the looser my understanding of the word 'happy'. Is there such a thing as a happy man? What if I had refused? Would I have spent my life watching my family crumble, wishing that I had taken on the security of the job which would at least have ensured that we didn't starve? Would I have left this place and learnt something else, and perhaps had a different life altogether? I think of my adiyaan, the young one who worried me because he didn't fit … He finally left Nagercoil and Parvathipuram, and he learnt a trade, became a carpenter. He lives far away, in Andhra, and he married a woman there. I wonder if he is happy. He left on his own and made his own life.

But what struck me then was that no matter what I had chosen I would have found something to regret. And then came the question: is there something beyond regret? Since I would regret my life no matter what choice I made, was the regret something that was always inside me? Was I born with it?

That night I dreamt again, a different dream.

All around, as far as the eye can see, there are scaffolds. Each has a rope, a white rope that glows yellow in what seems to be flickering firelight, though I can see no fire anywhere. Under each scaffold is the well, and in each well is something …

I walk amongst the scaffolds, on uneven ground with patches of grass on it. When I look up the sky is dark, but the firelight on the ground seems to show black clouds above. A strand of fear flickers through my chest. Those are rain-clouds. It will rain soon. The rain will put out the fires, and then I will be alone in the dark.

As the fear grows I walk faster, but there is no end to the scaffolds, and no change in the light. Where is the familiar primer-coated door, I wonder.

Far away, from behind one of the uprights of a scaffold, steps a dark figure. He is a man, I can see, with a big moustache, the ends of which curl up and form circles under his eyes. His eyes are red, and contemptuous. He is bare-chested and wears a mundu in the old style, like trousers, with a sash. When I go closer, I see that he has a sword in his sash, a sword that he draws when I get near him.

His eyes flash with contempt and disdain when he speaks to me. 'Insect!' he thunders.

'Who are you?' I ask.

'The aratchar,' he replies. 'The real aratchar.'

'What do you mean, the real aratchar?'

'I kill for my king, without question, without feeling. Do you know what all these scaffolds are?'

'No.'

'They are my scaffolds. I have killed thousands, and I do not care.'

'Yes.'

'And you—you are a pretender!'

That strikes me as true. I do the job but in my heart I am only a farmer. 'Yes,' I say. The enormity of my deception strikes me then. I behave like an aratchar but my heart is that of a mouse. I am overwhelmed by shame, and then I come awake.

The shame lasted into wakefulness.

I had played with the writer, led him by the nose,

made him run around. And all along he was being more honest with me than I had been with him, even with myself. He had taken it all without protest, and kept coming back for more. In some ways he was more mature than I had been so far.

What was I doing? Why couldn't I drop the pretence? I was not really the man he wanted to write a book on. Why did I want to force my writing on people?

Next time the writer comes, I thought, I will speak to him. I will tell him I cannot bear this. I will give him the books and tell him that the book does not matter, that my life does not matter, and kick him out of my life.

As I decided this the rain began again, driven by a strong wind from the south with the taste of the sea on it. It rattled on the tiles with great force and opened a leak in the kitchen roof through which a large drop plopped loudly down on the floor every half-minute or so. I got up in the dark, found my way into the kitchen, and lit a match. I put a pot on the floor under the leak but the noise of the drop falling was louder than before and I feared it might wake Chellammal. I found the rag with which she wiped the floor and left it in the pot, and the sound softened.

I'd never done something like this before. I would normally have woken Chellammal up and told her to do it. Why was I doing it?

Because of the shame, I thought. I had been a pretender.

Now I knew what I had lost when I became a hangman, at least some of it. I had lost my innocence, I think, and my self-respect.

I couldn't sleep then, not with all this going around in my mind, and I considered what I would say to the writer when he came next. Then it occurred to me that if I refused to do the book and sent him away I would have to go back to the old life, the old rut. Would I be able to do that?

No, I wouldn't, for I wasn't the person I'd been before the rains. A new feeling arose for the writer. He must have known that this would happen. He was the one who had brought this on me. I would confront him next time, and show him what his interference had cost me.

Damn the man, I thought, as I turned over to ease the ache in my legs.

A pretender, that's what I was.

And so was the writer.

18

He came in the morning, in the rain, with his umbrella, and at the gate he grinned moistly at me, rainwater dripping off his beard. The sight was funny and I was tempted to laugh, but instead I glared at him.

'What's the matter?' he asked. 'Why do you look so grim?'

'Do I look grim?' I asked sarcastically.

He took off his wet glasses and polished the lenses with his kerchief. Without his glasses he looked younger, more ordinary, vulnerable, and a little tired. His eyes were turned inwards, like Ramayyan's at his prayer, and when he had wiped his lenses clean and put the spectacles back on his nose I could see how they hid his real expression. Or was this more deviousness, this polishing of his glasses, to let me have a glimpse of his vulnerable side? I didn't know.

'Look,' he began, 'if I've done something wrong or

stupid, or something that hurt you, I'm sorry, okay? Just tell me what I can do to make up, and I'll do it.'

'I'll tell you what you can do to make …' I began.

For the first time since we met, he interrupted me. 'First tell me what I have done, otherwise what I have to do will not make sense.'

A wave of irritation swept over me. All morning I'd waited for this moment, planned what I was going to tell him, and here he was, spoiling everything. 'I'll tell you what I want to tell you,' I said, 'and you just shut up and listen to me.'

'Fine,' he replied. 'I'm listening.'

'Do you know what you've done to me?' I snapped at him. Some of the pent-up anger was showing.

'I don't,' he said. 'I wish you'd tell me.'

'You've come into my life, turned it upside down … My wife hardly talks to me since you came, do you know that?'

'I gave you the money that got you drunk,' he said. 'That much I know, and also that you were brought home in the small hours after that. I don't blame her for not liking that.'

'It's not just that, and you know it.' I paused to collect my arguments. They had sounded very good when I tried them out before dawn, but were failing now.

'So tell me what it is,' he said.

'You made me think,' I told him. 'You made me dig in my mind and now old matters consume me. They leave me restless, unable to sleep. I have nightmares. Do you understand?'

'I do,' he replied. 'When you write a book you have to dig in your mind. Otherwise you don't get a good book.'

'Why didn't you tell me?' I said. I realized suddenly that I was shouting, that my forehead was wet with sweat. 'Why didn't you tell me when I started?' I asked, in a more reasonable voice.

'I did tell you.'

'You didn't,' I snapped. 'You never told me that I'd go back years in my mind and rake up old troubles.'

'I told you it's not going to be easy.'

'Yes, you did. What you didn't tell me was that it was going to turn my life upside down and make everyone in the house unhappy, that it would make me drive my friends away—do you know that I no longer go out with them in the evenings as I used to?'

'Would you have believed me then if I had told you?'

'No … Not if you told me the way you did. You told me all this the way you would say that if you drop a glass tumbler it might break.'

'If I had told you more strongly, you would have kicked me out … And in any case, why did you decide to write? You could have left the writing to me, just answered my questions, spent a few days with me.'

'Nonsense,' I snapped again. This man was the limit. 'You're a dishonest man.'

'Dishonest?'

'Dishonest. That's why you left that pen with me, so that I'd owe you something: you did that on purpose, when I said that we'll see about the money later. If I'd just talked to you I'd still have had to go through all this. I'd have had to follow your roadmap through my mind and might have ended up even worse than now. Don't tell me you don't know that.'

'I do,' he replied. 'I do. But then there would have been no book if I hadn't done what I did.'

'Good,' I snarled. 'There would have been no book, and you wouldn't have got your money, and I would have lived on in my peaceful little world.'

'Peaceful it's not,' he said, 'and you know it.'

'Don't argue with me,' I said. 'You have no right.'

'I do,' he said. 'I've come here and put up with you and all your habits for the sake of seeing what's in your mind. Do you understand that?'

'I don't care … You shouldn't have come.' The anger had me firmly in its grip, especially now that he was trying to justify himself.

'All right,' he said. 'I shouldn't have come. I shouldn't have lied to you. I shouldn't have misled you. I shouldn't have given you that pen. So where do we go from here?'

'There's only one thing to do,' I said.

'Yes,' he said. 'There's only one thing to do.' He said something then that took my breath away with its impudence. 'Finish the book.'

'Out!' I said, when I could speak again. My voice was tight with anger, and when I pointed at the gate my finger trembled. 'Get out of my house and don't come back.'

'What did I do wrong?' he asked. Devious man.

'Nothing. I won't discuss it. Just leave. Just leave an old man in peace.'

He saw the fury in my eyes and began to walk towards the gate. 'Look, are you sure about this?' he asked.

'Just go,' I said. Then something struck me. 'Wait! There's something that you must take with you.' I went into the house and brought out the books, all of them, and the pen, and gave them to him. He took them miserably, and then, out of habit, he took a plastic bag out of the canvas bag that he always carried, and wrapped the books in it to prevent them getting wet.

'Don't do this,' he said. 'I'll leave. You keep these. You'll need them.'

'Damn you and your books,' I said. 'Take them. Just take them and leave. I don't want to see them again and I don't want to see you again.'

'Okay,' he said.

He looked crestfallen then, and I felt a moment's pity that I crushed because he deserved none. It would be best this way. 'Keep going,' I said. 'Don't come back.'

'Okay,' he said. 'Whatever it is, I wish you all the best.' He looked at the pack of books in his hand. 'There's probably enough here for me to write my book anyway. May I send you half the money?'

'Just go,' I said. 'Don't come back. Get out of my life.'

'Okay.' He turned and walked down the muddy path. At the corner he stopped and looked back at me, gave a sort of wave. I was tempted to wave back but instead I turned my back on him and walked into the house hoping never to see him again.

Chellammal asked, when I went in, 'Why did you send him away?'

'Because he caused too much trouble,' I told her.

'But you were also happy for some time,' she said.

'You were the one who complained about him,' I snapped.

'Yes. But will you be as you were from now on?'

I didn't answer her, for I myself didn't know. I didn't tell her that I'd been asking myself that same question over and over and over again.

19

That evening I went back to Murugan's, where the usual crowd collected.

I drank my coffee and listened avidly to the first bits of news. Someone's thatch roof had been blown off in the rain. Someone else had had a tree fall on their house, breaking a few tiles and opening the house to the rain. The tiles were impossible to fix in this weather, so he had to abandon the house. Other people had been flooded out of their houses. And the worst of the rains were yet to come.

By the time I was through with the coffee a certain detachment had set in. None of the talk stirred me as it had before. I was no longer a part of this. I heard the conversation but didn't listen. I tried to be interested in their little games and jokes, and I heard all of them without being touched.

I was a different man from what I had been before. I decided that it was perhaps because I hadn't been here in the evening for many weeks. If I hung around for a while, if I tried, I could go back to the old days, so I bought another coffee and waited for the feeling of belonging to return.

It didn't. Through that grey, wet evening, the detachment grew. Towards the end I found myself wondering how I'd ever been a part of this noisy, thoughtless group. Their talk grew wearying and I had to restrain my impatience a couple of times. Towards six I got tired and left.

Perhaps a drink would help.

I went that evening to Mahalingam's, and this time the man asked me no questions about how I'd pay. I had no money, I'd find some later, somehow. It didn't really matter. This time, too, he brought out the arrack and the boiled eggs. The first sip of the first glass went down smoothly enough, but from then on I didn't like it. By the end of the first glass I was feeling the same detachment as before, and I knew it wouldn't work.

I couldn't go back. I no longer belonged.

When I told Mahalingam I'd had enough he reacted as I'd thought he would. 'But why are you leaving so early?'

I couldn't very well tell him the truth. 'Headache,' I mumbled.

'What you get here is the best headache cure known,' Mahalingam said, laughing softly at his own joke. 'It postpones the headache to next morning.'

'Don't feel like it today.'

He looked at me strangely. 'You must be really ill,' he said, 'if you don't feel like a drink.'

'I must be,' I said. 'How much?' When he told me, I said, 'I'll pay you later.'

His face changed. 'The last time I gave you credit you promised you'd pay next day, but you paid after three weeks, after I reminded you several times.' He had actually cut off credit, but he didn't say so. 'Then you promised you wouldn't take credit again, and when I saw you with the money last time I thought you meant to keep your promise. Now I know you don't.'

'Shut up,' I said. I'd had enough of the man and his complaints. 'I don't have the money. I'll pay you when I have some and you can either wait for then or do what you like.'

I felt a tap on the shoulder. It was Murugan. He had just come in, after closing his shop for the day. 'What's the matter?' he asked.

Mahalingam rumbled, 'He wants credit. He's got no money.'

'I'll pay,' Murugan offered. 'How much?'

'Eighteen rupees,' Mahalingam said.

Murugan put two ten-rupee notes on the table. 'Take this,' he told Mahalingam, 'and shut up.'

'Thanks,' I said to Murugan. 'I'll see you tomorrow morning.'

'Whenever you like,' he replied.

That night again I dreamt of the man with the mask. But this time again the dream was different.

I saw the stone steps leading into the well below the

trapdoor. There was some flickering light from flames that I could not see, but at the foot of the steps it was still pitch dark. I felt the chill wind, heard the throbbing drums. I looked around for my adiyaans. They were there, and this time there was Ramayyan with them. Then they were all gone, and I saw the hundred and seventeen men in masks, flat masks. They too vanished, and then I was alone with the one man in the mask standing on the trapdoor, his arms and legs now free. His eyes, baleful and derisive, blazed with the same bright light as before.

I felt his iron hands tighten around my neck. I closed my eyes, and this time as I sank to my knees, I heard laughter, mocking laughter, from the dark in the well. I didn't know how, but it mocked me, and despite the breathlessness, with my heart threatening to explode in my chest, I felt a terrible guilt within me.

What have I done, I said to myself.

When I woke up, my first thought was a continuation of the dream: what have I done?

Why did I send him away, the writer? My work was incomplete. I had begun to talk openly of matters I had never shared before, not even with Maash, safe in the knowledge that someone would read my thoughts and continue his friendship with me … Without working on that book, without opening my heart at least a little, my days seemed incomplete and empty.

I must get those notebooks back now, I thought. I must.

A moment of blank panic took me. How would I get in touch with him?

Then I remembered. He had written down his address for me in the book, the old 1966 diary. I would go to Murugan early in the morning and buy a postcard. I would get the postman to write the address. I would only ask the writer to give me back the notebooks I gave him. Then I went back to sleep, and did not wake until seven.

At Murugan's shop at half-past-seven there was already a small crowd, a group of men on their way to work. Two were plumbers from nearby, and one carpenter from elsewhere, a stranger. I asked Murugan for tea, and while he was preparing it I asked him for a postcard. 'To whom will you write?' he asked.

'Nobody you know,' I replied sharply. It was none of his business.

'Not to the fellow who came here with you once, wanting something translated into Malayalam?'

I felt a stab of surprise and fear. How had Murugan guessed? 'What do you mean?' I asked.

'He passed this way a couple of days back. He left this with me, and told me to give it to you if you came looking for a postcard or anything of the kind.' From somewhere below he drew a packet.

The notebooks. The pen.

The pity I had felt for the writer and crushed when he left returned for a moment with great force. Then my heart lifted and I burst out laughing. He must have known. He must have known that I had changed for ever. From what he'd read earlier he must have figured out that I bought postcards from Murugan, that I had his address, and that in a few days I would write to him asking for the notebooks.

He must have been through the same thing at some time.

'What about the money?' I asked. 'You paid for me yesterday.'

'He gave me some … He left it with me when he left the packet. Don't worry about it.'

'Did he give it to you to give me with the packet?'

'No. He just told me to keep it … But you can have it if you want.'

Murugan knows me from his childhood, and I can't imagine him lying to me. If Murugan said the writer gave it to him for himself, it must be so. 'No,' I said. 'Thanks anyway, for the money and for keeping this.' I held the packet up for him to see.

'Yes. That writer fellow … He seemed sure you'd come. He bought a postcard, put his address on it, and told me to post it when you picked up the packet. Do you want to write something on the card? I'll mail it today.'

'It doesn't matter,' I said. 'This packet is what matters, he should know I've taken it, that's all.'

20

When I got back home and began to unwrap the books, Chellammal was sitting in the doorway, cutting vegetables. She lifted her head when I came in and noticed the packet. 'What's that?' she asked.

'The books,' I replied shortly.

'So you're going to write again.'

'Yes. I hope so.'

'Did the writer send them back?'

'No. He left them with Murugan.' I explained what he had done.

She laughed a belly laugh, the rough deep laughter of an old woman. 'He knew. He knew you better than you knew yourself.'

'Yes.'

'I think it's better this way,' she said. 'Keeps you occupied.'

I unwrapped the books, and opened the one I'd used last. Slowly I put down whatever had happened after I sent the writer away—the dream and the drinking and the detachment I'd felt in Murugan's shop. I took the rest of the day over it and went to bed light-hearted, if tired. I woke up next morning in the same light mood, but it worsened as the morning progressed. There was nothing to write, and I could feel the blackness rising again.

It grew intense as the morning passed, until I could feel it as a physical pain in the chest. The rain came heavily down, and unable to go out, I paced the house, upsetting Chellammal.

Pain. A memory surfaced, of a trip long ago to a place nearby, Thuckalai. It is not far from one of the older palaces of the king of Travancore, the Padmanabhapuram palace. It is a large, sprawling building, now a museum, and I cannot imagine how anyone could have lived in its high-ceilinged rooms with the long panelled corridors connecting them.

There were several memories, all intertwined. I recalled three of them clearly. One was of a conversation with Maash. The second was of a hall in a palace, and the third of a conversation with a smiling prison warder. They were all connected, by pain.

~

'You wouldn't believe the amount of thought that has gone into the art of causing of pain,' Maash said once, his voice roughening in anger. We were talking about the king and his prisons. 'There were people who specialized in the destruction of the human will.'

'I've seen some of these things,' I told him. I had come across something in the prison during my early years as a hangman.

'What?' he asked.

'The mukkali.' The mukkali was a tripod that the jail staff used at one time to keep recalcitrant prisoners in order by flogging them. In the days of the British, judges could sentence prisoners to be flogged: that at least has stopped now. I found out about the frequent use of the mukkali quite by accident. Once in a while I came into contact with a warder who had been sent to help us set up the scaffold, and sometimes there was the opportunity to talk a little. One afternoon, before Independence, I heard a shriek from the compound. The warder told me that it was a man being flogged.

'Can't he take it like a man?' I asked, not knowing that in flogging, as in hanging, there is ritual and purpose.

In the midst of his grim work the warder took off his peaked cap and wiped the sweat off his forehead. 'Don't you know it's a test?' he said.

'Who's being tested?' I asked.

He smiled, amused. 'Both, actually.'

'What do you mean, both? Who are the two?'

'The man with the cudgel and the prisoner. It isn't only about how well one can take pain, it's also about how much of it the other one can give and how expertly. The louder the prisoner shouts the better it is for the other fellow. If the prisoner doesn't scream in pain it means the fellow flogging him isn't doing justice to his job.'

'Why not?'

'Each time we flog someone it's like a little ceremony. We try to make sure all the prisoners see the flogging—and hear the prisoner's screams—so they know exactly what it means. If they know what they have to suffer maybe they won't break the rules.'

'Where do you hit him?' I asked.

'We take his pants down,' the warder explained, 'and expose his buttocks. When we hit him with the cane, we try to lay the strokes side by side: not overlapping, see, but side by side, with as little gap as possible. That's the most painful way.'

When I related this to Maash, years later, while explaining the mukkali to him, he shook his head in disgust and said, 'That's nothing. They were much more inventive than that. There was this infamous cage, the kazhuvanthooku, made of strips of iron with gaps in between of about an inch. They locked the prisoner into this narrow cage and left him out in the sun where the vultures came.

'Vultures look for movement, and they wouldn't see any because the man in the cage couldn't move. He couldn't even scream, because they gagged him. So when they left the man in the sun, the vultures followed soon. They pecked at him through the gaps with their heavy beaks, tearing off strips of his flesh until he died.

'Then there were man-sized frames full of spikes: they'd put people into those frames so they bled to death, pierced all over. There were needles fixed in those frames to put people's eyes out.

'All this was in the name of the king, mind you, and the king did it in the name of the lord ...'

'It's difficult to imagine all this,' I said.

'You can see it all for yourself,' he said. 'Don't imagine it. Go to Thuckalai, and from there to the Padmanabhapuram palace. There's a room full of these horrors for you to see.'

I have come here on the advice of Maash, and I stand open-mouthed at the contents of the hall. We spoke of this some time ago, and I have finally found the energy and the time and the money—for the bus fare—to come and see this palace. There is a hall of horror in the palace, just like Maash said there is. There are signs beside all the exhibits, explaining what each of them is for. They are all well-made, the exhibits: the blacksmiths who made them must have gone to great lengths to make sure they worked perfectly. And there are notes that explain how they work, and how to get the most out of them.

The kazhuvanthooku is rusting, the spots of rust looking like spots of blood in the diffused sunlight from the windows. The condemned man would have seen everything happening to him until the vultures got to his eyes. I can stand the exhibition no more. I leave that display of brutality behind and go out into the bright sunshine where I stand blinking in relief.

21

I remember returning from the palace disgusted at the king.

There is pain in nature: our generation saw enough of that. Kings had to inflict some on their enemies, that too was without doubt. But to make a science of the infliction of pain, and to use it under the guise of governance, that was a different matter. It left me disturbed and restless. I understood a little of farming, of cultivating the earth, of nourishing it: my ancestors, at least some of them, had been farmers, and it was in my blood. I understood the seasons, and that death was inevitable, but this was too much for me. The thought of having served a king whose tradition included such torture revolted me. I went straight back to Maash that evening. I caught him a little late, just before dark, and we walked together until we were just around the corner from his house.

I think Maash has been waiting for me to bring up the subject of the museum. A little smile plays about his lips, a smile that says, 'You should have believed me.'

I should have. 'I went to the palace,' I tell him. 'Everything was as you said it would be. Machines of pain.'

'You wouldn't have lasted a day as a hangman a few centuries ago,' he says. 'You're too soft.'

'Why do you say so?' I ask.

'The king's first hangmen were his own picked men. They did what they were told to, they had no problems of conscience or morality. They were grim men, those executioners.'

'What kind of men were they?' I ask.

'They would have been picked from among the fiercest of the king's soldiers. But no true soldier, no soldier with an ounce of soldierly spirit in him would kill a helpless man. But there were enough soldiers without such a spirit, and from among the bravest of them the king picked his bodyguards. From among the coldest of his bodyguards he picked his executioners.

'They were proud of what they did, for it was the only way they could get close to the king. That was important—being close to the king was like being close to god, and no matter what you did for a living it meant that you had status among the people. That was what it was all about. Power. Not very different from now, is it?'

'I don't understand,' I say. 'I've never thought about it.'

'The hangmen and the soldiers displayed their power. They liked it because they earned the respect—

or at least the fear—of the people. The king liked it because when these displays were within limits they consolidated his power …'

'What kind of displays are you talking about?'

'Public executions. Do you remember what I said about Marco Polo, and elephants?'

'Yes.'

'Those executions were held in public. People were free to come and watch the spectacle of somebody being killed.'

I can't imagine that. When I go for a hanging there might be a few visitors, the odd high official or politician, but most of the people around are there because it's their job. Very few people come to watch a hanging otherwise. Even with a small audience I have trouble. I avoid their eyes. If I were doing it in public … 'I don't think I could hang someone in front of a thousand strangers,' I say. 'Not even to feed my children.'

He looks at me, bright-eyed. 'See what I mean?' he asks. He becomes wistful. 'I wish we could talk inside the house, but you know how it is.'

'It's fine by me standing here,' I tell him. 'I just hope you won't get into trouble.'

'I'm already in trouble,' he grins. Even in the dark I can see what he must have been like as a small boy.

'May I ask,' I say, unable to hold back my curiosity, 'why you married her?'

The grin disappears. For a moment his face is bleak, and then he smiles crookedly. 'The usual thing,' he says. 'My father was progressive but not sensible, so when it was time for my sister to marry there was nothing we could give her as a dowry. I married my wife because she brought a dowry which went straight to my sister … The sad thing is that my sister was equally miserable. She passed on last year.' He shakes his head, as if to clear it. 'So you wouldn't be able to hang someone in public.'

'I don't think so.'

'The king's executioners not only hanged people in public, they did it with much haste and very little care. They didn't have a gallows, as you do. They used the nearest convenient tree and the nearest convenient rope, and they went out of their way to make the death as unpleasant as possible so that the audience would know what happened to those who brought the king's displeasure on their heads.'

'I wouldn't do that,' I say. I could never do that, no matter how big the rewards. Of that, at least, I am sure.

'Those hangmen used to boast of their prowess … There was a diwan, Velu Thampi Dalavar, who was notorious for having faced up to the British. They say he was a good administrator, that he dispensed his own form of justice. He had his own people, and he travelled and investigated serious crimes and delivered punishment on the spot … But it was all part of the same thing. His hangmen too loved boasting about the number of men they had hanged.'

'I can't imagine that.'

'Well, Velu Thampi suffered at the end. The British surrounded him, and it is said that he killed himself to avoid capture. They brought his body back to

Trivandrum and strung it up for people to see … One of the few occasions when the British showed their true colours. They were the same as the kings, only more experienced—you see, there was no difference. Our kings were fools, the British were cunning, and the people were too stupid to do anything for themselves, brainwashed by their rulers and their scriptures.'

As Maash says this a picture of Ramayyan arises in my mind, speaking at dusk in the temple about trying to do what the scriptures say, and not being able to do it. 'The only man with whom I talk of the holy books is Ramayyan Gurukkal,' I say. 'He doesn't seem to be brainwashed.'

Maash looks sharply at me. 'I'm not saying that the holy books are not good. There is wisdom in them. But what do they say? Obey your king. Obey your parents. Obey your elders. Don't they say that?'

'Yes, they do.'

'Do they tell you, think about good and bad and do the good?'

'I don't think so … When I spoke of this to Ramayyan he said I had to find my own dharma.'

'Aha!' he exclaims. 'See? See what I mean? Ramayyan is honest, and he tells you the truth. But if he had wanted to mislead you he could have done it. You would have believed it, wouldn't you, if he made up some nonsense for you to follow?'

I would have. I think I understand what Maash has been saying. I have to find my own way. Perhaps there is no one who will guide me. Fear grips me: I am lost.

22

Looking back, Maash seemed to think that power meant the capacity to inflict pain. He used to keep saying that power in this country is based on the capacity to create trouble. It's not the best who wins, but the one who can make the most trouble.

I have never thought deeply about these matters but I cannot imagine inflicting pain on the scale that he spoke of. But in the light of what he had said, I can make sense of the dream in which the man called me a pretender. If he was something like Velu Thampi's followers, I am a pretender.

The pain I inflicted on condemned men was out of ignorance, not desire. Did the condemned man really suffer it? Was his last memory the memory of pain? What were his last moments like?

I did not know, and I tried hard to remember particular hangings to see if I had an answer to that one. The condemned man is a youngster, barely into his twenties. He is my first ever victim, so to speak: he is actually the king's victim and it is just my job to deliver the king's punishment.

He is a mere boy, no more than twenty years old, and he is soft and unhealthy from the regimen in the condemned cell: he has had no exercise for months, and he eats poor food. He is pale from lack of sunlight, and his body is slack. He has shaved the previous evening and his skin is soft and smooth, making him look even younger and more vulnerable than he is.

The dark is beginning to lift and the stars are fading out of the sky. Soon there will be the morning's mist, but before it descends my work will be done.

I wait at the scaffold. The warders lead him into the gallows enclosure and on to the trapdoor, and one of the adiyaans places his feet in the centre of the trapdoor. The rope is ready: one end is hitched to the hook on the side of the eastern upright, and at the other end is the noose, with a slip knot that I tied with fingers that trembled.

The king still reigns, and the prison warders are his men. They carry no firearms, though most of them are armed with canes that they are prepared to use mercilessly if necessary: four of them would have gone into the condemned man's cell to get him out, ready for trouble. They surround him still, watchful, not overtly menacing, but making it clear that he won't get away.

The adiyaans tie his hands behind his back, and his ankles together as he stands on the trapdoor. They lower the mask on to his face. His last view will be that of the unpromising wall in front of him, and of a few men in uniforms. By first light he also, perhaps, can make out the door through which his body will go.

As a last look on earth, it leaves much to be desired. I wonder, what would he like to see last?

On the condemned man's last day they indulge him as best they can. He meets his family, if he wants to, on his last evening. He eats what he desires. He gets spiritual or religious advice from a priest of any denomination he chooses. After all that, to leave looking at that wall and the little door and the uniforms . . .

As I bring the knot round to its position under his ear I remember the look in his eyes before the mask came down. His face in that moment was strangely relaxed. Not just his face, his whole body. His eyes, I had noticed, were turned inwards, and I thought: though he looks at the wall he does not see it.

What does he see?

The mask is down, the noose is tight, and the superintendent gives the signal. I pull the lever, the man disappears into the well, and there is the thud of the door hitting the padding beneath. The rope quivers for a never-ending moment, and then it is still.

He is gone, but the question remains: what does he see as he goes? Does it help him with his pain, his last sensation?

I asked Maash about this one evening. I described the wall, and the uniforms, and the little door in the corner.

'This is what he looks at,' I said. 'But what do you think he sees?'

'I don't know,' Maash had replied. 'Ghosts, perhaps.'

This was all I could remember. I wished the writer was back. I didn't feel like writing him a letter, though I would have liked to have him around to bully a little, to listen to some of his words that made no meaning. He was so different from Maash. Perhaps I would write him.

No, I thought, having the writer around would be an indulgence. I would walk with him and talk with him and his presence would lighten my mood, but I didn't think it would help me write.

I wished I'd asked Maash what he meant by that cryptic one-word answer: Ghosts. He rarely said anything that didn't have some meaning.

Despite the rain, I went for a walk.

Again it came, in a little rush, a burst of words. This wasn't a memory, just a kind of quiet understanding.

Maybe the boy *was* seeing ghosts. Every man whom I hanged had in his own time murdered at least one other person. They didn't give death sentences for murders committed in a moment of uncontrollable anger or in self-defence. They gave death sentences to those who planned their killings, or killed cruelly or wantonly, or killed a policeman. So every man I hanged had been responsible for at least one death, a planned killing.

The man would have spent at least a few months, in the early days, before Independence, thinking about what he had done and why he had done it. Afterwards the months would have lengthened into years with the various processes of appeals. Years in the condemned cell, with the shadow of death over him … And all this while he would have had nothing to do but confront his crime.

If the man were an ordinary kind of man, like me, he would have regretted it. He would have regretted it from the bottom of his heart, and he would have had to live with that regret the last few months or years of his life. It would have weighed him down, and blackened his soul.

No wonder their eyes turned inwards when they came to the scaffold. Perhaps to such men the pain would not matter.

~

Raghavan Nair is a big man, tall and heavily-built, an imposing presence in his white uniform shirt with the Ashok Chakra on his epaulettes. He is a strong man, with a back that he learnt to keep ramrod straight during his stint long ago with a Viceroy's Commission in the Indian Army.

He is unusual in that he does not stand on ceremony and is willing to talk to anybody. Even I have had a few conversations with him, though he is far above my status.

When there is a man in the condemned cell, Raghavan Nair visits him at least once every day, and has a few words with him. He told me this himself soon after he became superintendent, and I have wondered why.

I ask him the question only after I am sure that he will not take it amiss that a humble hangman wants to know why he talks to the condemned man every day. His answer is straight. 'The man is suffering,' he says. 'He has to spend his days facing himself and what he has done, and I pity a man who has nothing to do but that. I speak to him to ease his loneliness.' He pauses for a moment to collect his thoughts, and adds, 'Maybe it comes as a relief, the end.'

That must be true, I thought, with a lift of the heart, when I remembered the conversation and wrote it in the notebook. If the superintendent of the prison, a high official, one who had supervised a few dozen executions himself, one who had spoken to several dozen condemned men at least once a day said this much, it must be true. The end was deliverance, regardless of the pain.

But a few minutes later there was another memory, of a prisoner who refused a priest. I had seen only part of what happened, but Raghavan Nair had seen it all, and he told me about it afterwards.

The condemned man is a Christian named James.

The previous night he asked for a priest, and within a few hours one is available. But when the priest goes to the condemned cell at four on the morning of the execution, the prisoner doesn't want to see him.

'There's nothing for you to do here, Father,' he tells the priest.

'Let me pray with you,' the chaplain pleads. 'Your last prayer.'

'No, no, Father,' James insists. 'No prayer. It's not time yet. Go away. Leave me alone.'

The rituals are over. James has bathed, he has eaten well the previous night, and the trouble is unexpected. Several warders led by a sub-inspector go warily into his cell. 'Come,' the sub-inspector says. 'You know it's time.'

'Time for what?' asks James.

'Time for you to say your prayers,' answers the warder.

'You're going to hang me, aren't you?' asks James.

'I'm afraid so,' replies the warder.

'I'm not coming,' the man says. And he refuses to budge.

The warder goes to his chief, the superintendent. Raghavan Nair is the superintendent, the man whose responsibility it is to get the man on his way with as little trouble as possible. The superintendent is aware that time is passing, that the man must be hanged soon, and he makes his way to the condemned cell. He can always put a group of six warders in the cell and order them to bring the prisoner out by force if need be, but he would prefer not to do that to a condemned man on his last morning. His intention, because he doesn't want to use force, is to persuade the man to come on out to the scaffold, and he thinks he can do it, for he has made it a point to see the prisoner each day.

Raghavan Nair's first attempt to get James out of his cell meets the same reaction. 'You've spoken to me every day I've been here,' James tells him. 'You know I'm not a bad man. I've done nothing to you. Why are you so intent on killing me? What have I done to you?'

'Let's talk awhile,' Raghavan Nair says. 'But let's move on from here. We can talk as we go.'

'Why should I move on?' asks James.

Raghavan Nair then begins another part of the ritual: he reads out the list of crimes that James has committed. That seems to get through to the prisoner, who agrees to move onwards. He leaves the cell, and the two of them walk towards the gallows enclosure, followed by a contingent of ten wary warders, all with canes at the ready. James comes along, asking all along why they want to kill him when he hasn't done anything to them. In the enclosure he asks me, too, the same question, and I say nothing. Then his hands are tied, the mask goes on his face, and the noose round his neck. I tug at the lever, he disappears from sight, and the rope quivers briefly. Then he is dead.

~

'Why do you want to kill me?' the man had asked, standing on the trapdoor. What could I have said? The voice I heard wasn't that of a man relieved to go to his death. I remember the plea in his voice when he spoke to me. I had looked away then, but the question had stayed on in some dim pit of my mind and had arisen once again now to haunt me.

I was sure death was a release to many of the men I hanged, but not to all of them. In any case, it was a release only because those men had been stuck in a small barred room with nothing to do but count the cracks in the ceiling, and think of their crime and their death.

Also, whether they were relieved or not didn't alter my involvement in the hanging in any way. So what, I thought, and what was I trying to get at?

I gave up writing for the day and decided instead to read what I had written. Working on something over and over again usually only improves it. I put the current notebook away and brought down the first that I'd written.

I could see that this wasn't the book I had thought I'd write. What I had done didn't make a story at all. I had thought I would sit down with the pen and the notebooks and the words would come easily, but now I knew how rarely they came, and how painfully. If the writer could make a good story out of this he would be a very good writer, I thought.

The power failed and the bulb went off, leaving us in the dark. There was a glow from the embers in the kitchen, enough for Chellammal to find a matchbox and light the small kerosene lamp that was our standby when the power went off.

I hardly noticed what I ate that night, and when I had eaten I went to bed straight away. There was a great weariness in my bones. It was still there when I woke up the next morning, and it persisted past breakfast and into the afternoon.

Then a picture emerged.

This is one of my earliest hangings, and the man I will hang is from a village not far from my own house: thirty miles, perhaps; a day's walk.

Yesterday I lost my patience with one of the adiyaans who was a little slow tying the end of the rope to the hook on the upright of the gallows, and I spoke to him harshly. He did not like it—no lad of eighteen would like being rebuked in the presence of his peers and a group of officials—and today he is sulking. He does his job, but he does it deliberately, slowly. I think he is trying to irritate me. He doesn't succeed, because I have a tight hold on myself. I will speak to him afterwards, because indiscipline is harmful, but I will not lose my patience with him again.

He climbs down from the upright after fastening the rope to it, and we are ready. We hear the footsteps of the warders marching in step, surrounding the condemned man, and then the door opens and he is with us.

I get a good look at him. He is a tall man, and thin. His appeals were turned down very quickly so he has not had the time to get the fat, pale unhealthy look that men take on when confined for long in the condemned cell. His back is straight, and though he does not stare at anyone, he does not avoid my eyes.

His eyes are remarkably clear. He seems at peace. He has come to his death with dignity, and for a moment I am afraid of his enormous will, of the pride that lurks in those clear eyes.

I know why he is here: he killed two people. He comes from a wealthy family, wealthy enough to have a gun, a double-barrel gun that they use for hunting the wild boar that attack their farmland. The family have much land, most of it irrigated, all of it well-managed, and their sharecroppers respect them.

This man's brother was a man who liked to fight, and to drink. A dangerous combination. One night he got into an argument with a neighbour over a woman, the neighbour's wife. They had both had too much to drink. Hot words became blows and the brother beat the neighbour senseless. The neighbour went home that night, but the story goes that he returned three days later, with a trusted servant and a knife. He stabbed the brother dead and ran away.

There were no witnesses and the knife was never found. The neighbour got away with murder.

This man took the law into his own hands. He was patient, and he planned his revenge well. He found out that the neighbour visited another woman nearby at night, usually accompanied by the same trusted servant. One night he ambushed the two of them on their way to the woman's house. The neighbour got one bullet in the chest, the servant the second, in the head. But as it happened there was a second servant in the group that night, and above was a moon bright enough for him to recognize the shooter, who took long enough over reloading his firearm for the servant to get away.

In his own reckoning, the man has committed no crime: he has only settled accounts. If the law hadn't messed up the first case, if the law had been able to find the man who murdered his brother, he wouldn't have been here. In my heart I too feel that he has done the right thing. I will hang him all the same, just as if he has done what I consider utterly wrong.

I knew now why I was so short of patience at that hanging: I was angry at myself for having to do it. I was sure the man wasn't unhappy to die. I could see that in his eyes. He wasn't relieved, of course, but he didn't regret what he had done, not in the least. And I felt a sympathy for him that I never felt for any other prisoner.

I still regret having had to hang him; he did not deserve it. No law that failed to find his brother's killer had the right to send him to the gallows. But I performed the hanging in the name of the king, in the name of god. All hollow, as I discovered later, but when I did it I did it for the king.

The blackness gained weight. When I shut the notebook that evening, I felt utterly alone. Totally isolated, and now, it seemed, without any hope of ending that isolation.

23

With the rains now coming down heavily there was little work in the fields. I did go out walking a few times, but it was so unpleasant, with the slush and the rain slanting down in the wind, that I stayed indoors most of the time.

The weight of my executions, the weight of the pain I had caused the men whom I killed, the weight of the guilt of killing at least one man who had done no real wrong, all these burdened my mind. I could not eat, and sleep came rarely. I could not go back to my friends and my normal routine, or whatever I had considered normal before the writer came, for I was no longer part of it. I couldn't even go to Mahalingam's for a drink, I knew it would be useless.

There was a distance between Chellammal and me, but somehow she did not seem to mind. Most of the time I ignored her and sat with the books, but she continued to do for me whatever she always did.

I began to understand how I had changed. Before I started on the book I had been aware of many things about the house and about the weather. With a farmer's eye for the land and for the crop I had watched for changes in the weather, in the winds, and noticed the little creatures that came foraging in different seasons. After I started on the book I hardly noticed anything. I didn't notice the dog who had been my constant companion ever since he came: it surprised me sometimes to find him in his usual position, half asleep at my side. I even forgot my children and my grandchildren.

My vision had shifted from the fields outside to those inside my mind, and I still had no idea what I would find there. I did not know what I was looking for.

Day and night blurred into one. I lay awake sometimes, and sometimes I walked in the fields when the rain permitted, without seeing anything. Sometimes I ate what Chellammal put in front of me and at other times I ignored food. When people came to call me I smiled with my mouth and excused myself, telling them I was in no shape to go out. Murugan heard that I was ill and came visiting, to ask if he could get me something, but I sent him away: what I needed was beyond him.

I awoke early one morning, at first light, to shouts and went out to investigate. There was a boar in a trap, a pit dug at the edge of a field of tapioca. A crowd of men and boys, all of whom I knew, had collected around the pit. They would get the boar out of the pit and kill it and in the evening there would be a small feast. Killing wild boar was a crime, but the animals were pests: they came in the night and destroyed whole fields of crops, digging for roots.

Someone would call in the evening with a bit of curried pork. Some of them, I knew, wondered why I had disappeared from my usual haunts, and would perhaps try to tempt me back, but I wouldn't go.

As I trudged back home with my mind still on the boar I remembered another conversation with Ramayyan.

Dusk is the worst time of the day. All around I see people return home, tired from their day's work, and men gathering at coffee shops. A few youngsters are at the bus-stop, waiting to go to the cinema, and at the temple is a small crowd of worshippers.

I have just discovered that I am no longer the aratchar. The king's privy purse has been abolished. He has the wealth that his forefathers built up and the palaces and so on, but otherwise he has no privileges. And with the abolition of the purse, my job may come to an end. It is likely that I will have to hang no more men. It is a relief, but I feel that I have to do *something*. I do not know what, and I want to ask Ramayyan.

I wait for the crowd at the temple to pass, and when Ramayyan locks up the temple at half-past-six I go with him to his house. It is already dark. 'You know the rituals,' I tell him. 'You know all about penance. What's the penance for a hangman?'

He smiles. 'None,' he says. 'You've done nothing wrong.'

'But I feel the need for a penance.'

'What do you think you do during your puja here before each hanging?' he asks. 'You kill in the name of the king, or the government. You only need to do a token penance, and that you do beforehand.'

'Sometimes I feel that's not enough.'

'It is.' He calls to his wife for some water. 'I can see it from your point of view, but there is no penance for you because you have done no wrong.'

'Yes.' I'm irritated. 'So the book says. But I carry the burden and the burden hasn't read the book so it doesn't know that it has no place in me.'

He laughs. 'You're right, of course. Why don't you look at it differently?'

'Differently? How?'

'You know about farming, don't you?'

'Yes.'

'What do you feel when you kill something that might destroy your labour? A pig, say, that might lay a whole field waste?'

'Nothing. I'm defending my own livelihood, my family.'

'So you feel nothing when you trap a pig in a pit and you and your friends gather together and roast it and eat it and celebrate.'

'Nothing.'

'What if I tell you that the men you've killed were pests? They killed other people, mostly for money, sometimes for love, sometimes for honour or revenge. Don't you see that such people destroy the work of society?'

I think about it. 'I see them just before they die,' I say. 'At that time they are vulnerable. I cannot think of them as destroyers because when I see them they are pitiful creatures.'

'You know of the blood on their hands,' he says. 'Think of that and do your job.'

'But why me? Why should I be stuck with the job of the hangman?' I ask. This thought has been at the back of my mind always, and this is the first time I'm voicing it.

'That question has no meaning,' Ramayyan says. 'Why is the king the king? Why is the condemned man the condemned man? Why am I a priest? Why is anybody what he is? Who knows? It's just fate.'

'Fate?' I ask. This is something I hear often, and it means nothing because it is just another way of saying that we do not know. 'Nonsense.' The word just slips out, I do not normally use such strong language in conversation with Ramayyan. 'Sorry,' I add, 'I don't mean to offend.'

'I'm not offended,' Ramayyan says with a small, bleak smile. 'You just are who you are and eventually it makes no difference who you are because you're the same as anyone else. That's what the scriptures say and that's what I'd like to believe.'

'You've said this before,' I say. 'That's what you'd *like* to believe. Don't you believe?'

'The words make a sort of sense to me,' Ramayyan replies, 'but in my heart I don't believe. I can't believe. Not yet.' He smiles again, without the bleakness, and I can see the pain behind his eyes. 'Belief is hard.'

'Why do you say these things to me, things that you don't believe?' It infuriates me that Ramayyan replies from the holy books and says things he does not mean.

'Because I am trying to learn them myself.'

'I don't understand you.'

'I am sorry. That is my weakness. I try to answer your questions as best I can, and fail.'

'Then what use are the books?'

Ramayyan shakes his head. It is only then that I notice, in the lamplight, how much he has aged in the last few years. His hair has gone grey and his face gaunt, though his stocky body is still vigorous and his veined thick hands still strong. 'I don't know,' he says. 'I was taught as a child that they contain true things, and I believed it. I still do.'

'What true things?'

'That you and I are the same as that pig stuck in the pit.'

'How can that be?'

'I can't explain. I do not know it well enough to explain it to you.'

Ramayyan is my good friend, and I know that he speaks from the heart. I hear him out and leave, the weight still on my chest. As I leave I wonder about the holy books that Ramayyan reads. From what he says, they contain little of any use, except perhaps to people who spend many years with them. But a holy book must be simple, otherwise how can a man like me, or like most of the others I know, understand it? Does this mean that the holy books are only for a few? If there is a god he must have more sense than to create books that are only for some.

I don't understand the rituals, either, but I do them when I have to, and I will continue to do them. For there is nothing else to be done.

~

As I sat thinking about that conversation with Ramayyan I knew why I made all those visits to Sabarimala, and kept all those vratams. It was a penance. But it would never be sufficient because I didn't know what would be a sufficient penance. I remembered Maash's story about the shishya who burnt himself for considering the murder of his guru, and I knew exactly what the shishya had felt when he asked his guru what the punishment was; if the punishment was that he should burn himself, he could not but do just that—bury himself in the burning paddy husk and melt in the slow fire. I knew now why the king went through those rituals to absolve himself of the sin of killing a man. And when I thought about it a little more I knew something that I don't think the king knew: you had to find your absolution yourself, through your heart, and not through an empty ritual carried out by paid servants.

The king had been fooling himself, unless, of course, what he wanted was the appearance of absolution rather than the real thing. The superintendent was fooling himself too, and so was the messenger, and everyone else in the charade. Because in the end that was all it was: a charade. Only the hangman and the condemned man actually did anything.

The priests who did the rituals were also fooling themselves. There were a few, like Ramayyan, who had their hearts in their work, but the rest, they were all fooling themselves, just like the king. For them, too, it was just a charade.

And for me, too, for I did a few rituals—the vratams, the sacrifice of the rooster. Was I in a charade too? How could that be? The condemned man died at the end of what I did, so how could it be a charade? I tried to believe, I hoped there was a god who would accept my penance: was that a charade? Was all of life itself a charade?

I remembered Ramayyan saying that belief was hard. Like trust. Like faith ... Like life.

Death. Death was at the core of it. How could I have killed? How could I have taken away something that no one could ever return? How could I atone for having taken it so many times? The confusion grew, for all the truths I had learnt seemed to have been washed away, as if in a flood.

What was I doing?

I was tired, and I lay down. I felt no hunger or thirst, I lay still for a long while, until after sunset. Then, at Chellammal's insistence, I drank some tea. That night I slept early, and I dreamt again. It was the old nightmare in the beginning, but it was changed, and in its new form I didn't really know whether it was a nightmare at all.

I see the steps first, the irregular stone steps leading into the dark well below the trapdoor, but now they are very clear. I can see the patches of discolouration in the stones, and a few patches of slimy moss. All around is the soft darkness before the dawn, but when I look up there is only blackness, a blank darkness. There is light from flames that I cannot see, but it flickers, and the dark at the foot of the steps is still black and solid and shapeless.

From far away comes the sound of drums, rising and falling.

In the darkness of the well lurks the old menace. I stand on the uppermost step of the staircase and look down, and see a flicker of movement below, but it is gone as I see it. I turn from the well to look for reassurance in the familiar faces of my adiyaans, who a few moments ago accompanied me into the enclosure, along with the guards, and the man in the mask.

They are gone. I am alone. Completely alone. Everyone is gone. Even the man in the mask.

The drums fall silent, and all of a sudden I am on the trapdoor. There is no mask on my face, for I can see. I look down and see my bare feet in the centre of the trapdoor, and my legs, clad in the striped trousers of the condemned man. My arms are tied, and so are my ankles, though there is no one around who could have done it. When I look up I see the noose hanging above me, shining whitely. I have a fading memory of having tied my own knots.

How could I have tied those knots myself, I think, it's impossible. As I think this the ropes on my arms and legs seem to fall away and I find I can swing my arms and walk freely.

I must find out what lies in the well, I think. This time there is no terror. I will be able to run away if need be, so I am not afraid. I pause at the top of the steps, take a deep breath, and when I look down the blackness is still there, though the menace is gone. The flicker of movement I saw earlier is gone too.

I start slowly down the steps. They only appear rough: they are smooth and cool and dry beneath my bare feet. With each step I take the light comes with me, and the darkness recedes further.

At the bottom of the flight of stairs I stop. There is nothing in the well. The light is not particularly good but I can see that there is nothing here, just walls of cool mossy stone. In one corner is a small hole in the stone floor, a hole in which water glints. The warders say that there is always water in that hole, though there is no obvious source of the water.

I look around carefully, once again, and find nothing. I inspect the corners, and again find nothing. I have been running from nothing.

I turn my back to the well, and put my foot on the bottom step of the staircase. I pause for a moment, and a voice speaks in my mind: then I know that this is a dream, and that it doesn't matter. 'Why did you run from me?' the voice asks. 'All of you will come to me in the end anyway, you and the others. Didn't you know?'

Then I wake up, I come smoothly awake, wondering where my fear has gone, and how.

When I woke up I wasn't sure I was really awake. I looked around, and after a moment's confusion found the usual comforting signs of being home: the glow of embers fading in the hearth, the sharp tang of woodsmoke and ashes and damp cloth, the patter and squeak of a mouse exploring the kitchen, the scratch of the rough blanket on my arms and chest.

I became slowly aware of the soft drizzle, and the dark outside, the solid dark that comes on moonless, starless nights. It was sometime in the middle of the night, I didn't really care exactly what time it was. I was tired and bathed in sweat, as if a fever had just passed. There was a great thirst raging in my throat and I got up slowly to fetch some water. I discovered that despite the great weariness my body was light, that getting up wasn't as difficult as it had been lately. I drank my water, so cool that it seemed almost to cut its way through my throat. I put the pot silently back in its place and found my way back to bed. When I lay down again, I think I went to sleep the moment my head rested on the pillow.

I slept late that morning. There was a break in the rains when I opened my eyes and sunlight poured in through the open door. A breeze came up, and the clouds hid the sun again, but the rain stayed off. I must write down everything about the night, I said to myself, and send this off to the writer.

I sat down in the doorway with my notebooks after I had finished my morning coffee. Before lunchtime I had finished writing of the strange dream of the night, and when I was done I felt drained. Enough, came the thought, you've written enough, and I put the books away.

More rain-clouds came, grazing the trees on the hillsides, and with them came the dark. I ate my lunch slowly, and brought the books down for the second time that day. The emptiness persisted, and the thought came again, you've written enough: stop. Without opening them I held the notebooks I had grown so close to in these few months, and felt only a great relief.

I was through with them. I didn't want to read what I had written, I didn't even want particularly to see those books again. Time to call the writer, I thought. Then it struck me that he would have to travel a long way to get here, and I had nothing to give him other than these books. Easier, I thought, to mail the books to him.

I sat down and in the light of the bulb wrote a long letter to the writer, and put it in the last of the books. Then I put the books away, along with his pen, in a yellow plastic bag. 'All this is for that writer fellow,' I told Chellammal. 'I've got to send it off to him.' I picked up the bag but when I looked out of the door I saw that the rain had started again, which meant a walk to the post office in the slush. I'd do it later, there was no great urgency about it. There was no urgency about anything. There was a memory of urgency, a dim memory from long ago, but I knew that it was only a day old. Whatever it was, the urgency was gone. I just wanted to sit quietly and watch the world go past my doorway.

'Where are you going in the rain?' Chellammal asked when she saw me standing at the door, her voice rising in worry.

'Nowhere,' I told her, putting the bag back on the shelf, 'I'm going nowhere.'

Epilogue

By the time I was finished with the seven notebooks it was dark outside. I had read almost continuously for seven hours: I'd broken briefly a few times, for lunch, for tea, and then for a little walk down the lane to clear my head when some of the passages, written with effortless feeling, had filled me with envy.

This was the first time I'd read all of the hangman's journal in its complete form. What I'd read earlier had been bits and pieces from here and there, some of it translated, some of it in the original. It hadn't had that feeling of hanging together then. Now it did.

I understood many things now. I understood his son's anger at me, that his father had left his innermost thoughts to a stranger and not to his own son. He would carry that anger always, now that the hangman was gone.

The narrative had wound down midway through the seventh notebook and I was putting the little stack of books away in my bag before leaving for the railway station when a couple of sheets fell out of the last notebook. They were covered in his spiky handwriting and I thought for a moment that he had torn them out and thrown them away before retrieving them for me. But when I looked, I found they contained a letter from him. 'My foolish writer,' it began, and I smiled, and read on.

> 'I have done something I never thought I could do: I have written a book. Here it is, in these notebooks that you gave me. Here also is the pen you gave me: I return it because I cannot write another book.
>
> 'When we last met I was angry. But I know you will not hold that against me, because you know what it is to write a book like this one. I took back the notebooks from Murugan, as you thought I would, and I wrote what I had to. I opened many doors in my mind, and closed a few, and laid a few ghosts to rest.
>
> 'The first time you came, on that afternoon when you were mostly silent, you spoke of money. At my time of life I don't need any. Chellammal doesn't need any, either: we are all used to making do with what we have, and we will continue to do so. You keep the money. I know you must have spent a large portion of your advance making all those trips to Nagercoil and living in a hotel. I know now that you lived in a very poor hotel, one that you must have found uncomfortable, and I am a little sorry for having troubled you so. Only

a little sorry, though, for you did get my book out of all that trouble.

'As you can see, the book is not concluded. I do not know how to end it: the rest is for you to do. Although I am a great deal less preoccupied now, I do not have answers to my own questions, and I do not know what I will say if you ask me any. I also do not know if the pain and confusion that visited me while I wrote this book will return. Perhaps they will. Perhaps the forgotten memories I dug out will continue to haunt me. I do not know. I only know that at the moment I feel free, peaceful and I want this feeling to last.

'Come and see me if you have the time. Send me a copy of your book when it is done, even though I cannot read it. Perhaps you or your friend will find the time to translate it back into Tamil for me. Strange, isn't it, that I write a book that you will rewrite in another language, and translate back to my language so that I can make sense of it? I don't know if what I have done is what you had in mind when you first came here, or how much work you will have to put in to make it a book, but instinct tells me that you will try to keep it more or less as it is. I hope you succeed in that, for then it will be as much my book as it is yours.

'On one of the earliest occasions we met, you told me that writing this book would be painful for both of us. At that time I thought that the pain was all mine. Now I know otherwise. I know you have shared it, and have trusted me. Otherwise you would not have left these notebooks with Murugan.

'I do not know what else to say to you. Despite the anger, despite the quarrels, I liked having you around, and I must say I enjoyed baiting you. It is hard for me to admit this: I learnt something from you, though you are less than half my age and your head is full of useless book learning. I hope you find whatever it is that you look for, and that when you find it you discover that it is as good as you hoped for: you're not a bad fellow, though you do have a lot to learn.

Your friend and fellow foolish writer,
Janardhanan Pillai, aratchar'

~

The decision came on its own as I finished reading the hangman's last letter. A few minutes before I read it, as I packed for the way home, I'd been planning to rewrite the book, changing the chronology, adding my own research material as I went along, filling out a few characters, particularly the ones I knew, like Murugan, and Paraman, and so on. A little more on some of the mysteries in the lives of Maash and Ramayyan Gurukkal, perhaps, and something about the aratchar's five surviving children. A little character-building, an exposition of the writer's craft, of which I too was learning as I went along. Perhaps that was what my publishers expected: if they did, they were going to be disappointed, for they were going to get the hangman's jumbled and ragged story rather than a superficially more polished one from me.

As he wished.

Acknowledgements

The Hangman's Journal is based loosely on the life of Janardhanan Pillai, who became hangman for the king of Travancore in the early 1940s and, over three decades, performed 117 executions. While this book is a mixture of fact and fiction, and the protagonist is to a large extent my creation, my greatest debt is to Pillai.

My parents were, as always, very supportive through the writing of this book, and contributed a substantial portion of its historical content.

My old friend and former classmate from school, Prita, permitted me to share the book with her. Suresh, another old friend, read several versions of the manuscript and offered many valuable suggestions.

Several months of research went into this book. People who helped with the research include many friends and relatives: Mr P.R. Warrier, former Resident Editor of the *Matrubhumi*, without whose contacts very little would have been possible; Mr R.P.C. Nair,

Inspector General, Prisons; Mr Japamani, Superintendent, Poojapura Jail, and many of his colleagues; Mr K. Rameshan Nair, retired police officer and fellow-author; Mr P.S.M. Moideen, Director of the State Archives; Mr Ramananda Kumar, Nagercoil correspondent of the *Matrubhumi*; Mr Kumar, also of the *Matrubhumi*, who did a series of articles on the hangman in the eighties; Mr Raghavan Nair, who retired from the police force as Inspector General, Prisons, and who, despite the infirmities of age, gave me much useful information; Dr Alexander Jacob; and many others.

Support also came from my old friends Dinesh and Satish, and Chitra and Aditya.

The Hangman's Journal started with a letter from Ravi Singh, who commissioned the book, and who saw it through its various stages without losing patience.